# FINAL STOP
# ALBUQUERQUE

# ALSO BY ALICE ZOGG

*The Fall Of Optimum House*
*The Lonesome Autocrat*
*Tracking Backward*
*Turn The Joker Around*
*Reaching Checkmate*

# FINAL STOP
# ALBUQUERQUE

Alice Zogg

Aventine Press

This book is a work of fiction.

Published by Aventine Press
750 State St. #319
San Diego CA, 92101
www.aventinepress.com

ISBN: 1-59330-580-X

Library of Congress Control Number: 2009924966
Library of Congress Cataloging-in-Publication Data
Final Stop Albuquerque/Alice Zogg
Printed in the United States of America

*To my granddaughter Sarah and grandson Ryan*

*Someday you will be old enough to read this story*

# CREDITS

Many thanks to Sean Quinn of MB2 Raceway for graciously giving me a tour of the indoor Go Kart race course as well as answering my many questions about the sport. I also appreciate the permission received from Duncan Davis to use Go Kart racing information from his website. I am grateful to Kelly Peña for introducing me to her father, John Peña, former Mayor of Gallup, New Mexico, who kindly shared his knowledge about the Inter-Tribal Indian Ceremonial in Gallup. Again, like so many times before, Joan Joe helped with medical inquiries I had when writing this book. Richard Wagner at Harley-Davidson of Glendale, California came to my aid with information about motorcycles. Applause is due to my husband Wilfried for saying "yes" to our trip to Albuquerque during the balloon festival, enabling me to do some on-the-spot research. Once more, Valoise Douglas did a superb editing job. I appreciate all your help, Val! A thank you is in order to my computer-savvy daughter Andrea. When I made an error and was certain that I had ruined the entire manuscript, she was able to rescue it. Last but not least, I am indebted to my daughter Franziska for her continued commitment to proofreading my manuscripts.

# CAST OF CHARACTERS:

| | |
|---|---|
| **R. A. Huber** | Private investigator; sleuth par excellence |
| **Peter Huber** | R. A. Huber's husband; a writer |
| **Andi (Antoinette LeJeune)** | Huber's assistant; a dynamic young woman |
| **Elena Campione** | Andi's classmate; has disappeared |
| **Bruno Campione** | Elena's husband; a nightclub owner |
| **Ted Wilson** | Elena's father; a brilliant physicist |
| **Marcia Wilson** | Elena's step-mother; an attorney |
| **Kevin Wilson** | Elena's brother; a high school student |
| **Brenda Wilson** | Elena's sister; away at college |
| **Phil Drummer** | Nightclub manager; also serves as bouncer |
| **Rocky Santoro** | Bruno's employee; runs the newly acquired Arizona club |
| **Inger Santoro** | Rocky's wife; hates life "in the boonies" |
| **David Driscol** | Elena's ex boyfriend; still seems to hold a torch for her |
| **Ralph** | Hotel manager in Albuquerque; an observant fellow |
| **Celia Molina** | The Campiones' housekeeper; minds her own business |
| **Christine** | Elena's hair stylist; the gossiping kind |
| **Kirk Bergstein** | Wilson family estate lawyer; torn between loyalties |

# Prologue

Twenty-four-year-old Elena Campione watched in awe as the hot air balloons left the ground, beginning the Farewell Mass Ascension. This was the second wave of hundreds of balloons launched from Balloon Fiesta Park on the last day of the festival in Albuquerque, New Mexico. She gazed up into the dazzling array of colors filling the sky, captivated.

The young woman reflected on how glorious these last few days had been for her. She was lost in a crowd of thousands of spectators, and for once in her life she felt totally free. The "Special Shape" balloons launched early Friday morning had particularly caught her fancy. She had watched the balloon "characters" taking off from the ground and admired each one as it slowly joined the others in the sky. She recalled seeing a pair of bees holding on to one another, a two-story castle, an angel as well as a devil, two pigs and a cow. Her favorite was a stork holding a baby bundle in his beak.

Aware that her escape from reality would all come to an end soon, Elena sighed. She had made sure that no one followed her to Albuquerque, and she smiled secretively as she thought, *nobody is the wiser of where I'm at!* Why was it that people always made demands on her, she wondered. Her parents had held expectations that she could have never fulfilled. The pressures at college had been intolerable, and surely she could not be blamed for dropping out. Being married to Bruno had been wonderful, but now it turned out that even he was expecting too much of her. Grammy had been the only person who'd given her unconditional love, and she was dead. "Miss you, Grammy," she murmured into the on-looking crowd. If Elena had any qualms about shunning her responsibilities, they were pushed into the background of her mind as she enjoyed the moment.

When the final group of vibrant balloons glided into the distance, people around her started to disperse, but she stood and peered up into the firmament, mesmerized, until the vessels were nothing but specks in the distance. Then she turned around and … froze.

Recovering from the initial shock, she said, "What are *you* doing here?"

"Looking for you!" was the menacing reply.

# Chapter 1

Private investigator R. A. Huber was equally comfortable working out in the gym, on the dance floor, racing down the mountain on skis, dressed in a long gown at a black-tie function, or simply enjoying a game of chess. What made her unique, though, was how she chose to spend her golden years. Unlike most of her contemporaries who pursued hobbies or joined clubs after retirement, Huber had opened a private investigating business at that stage of her life. At first, family and friends had shaken their heads at her endeavor, but after she had solved some intriguing cases, even the most skeptical among them had to admit that the lady was good at detecting.

At the moment, she was fighting to keep her one-point advantage at a tie-breaker game of racquet ball. She had lost the first game 12 to 15, won the second 15 to 13, and the deciding one was now in progress at 11/10 in her favor. The scores ending in two digits for both players was an indication that they were well matched. However, Huber's opponent was ten years younger, a man, left-handed, and deadly.

At this stage of the game, Andi, the private eye's assistant, came in search of her boss and watched the end of the match. She was standing at the balustrade on the second floor of the gym looking down into racquet ball court number three. Andi was unfamiliar with the sport

and at first glance only observed that a small blue ball
was being hit by racquets, making it bounce off the walls.
Regardless, it only took a moment before she followed the
game with great interest and deduced that each player
had to get to the ball and swing at it before it bounced on
the floor twice. Huber had lost her serve and the man had
aced his, so the score was now 11 all. Soon it was 12/11
for her opponent and Andi realized that a person could
only score while being the server.

She hollered in her Southern drawl, "Gotta get your
serve back, Mrs. Huber!"

The lady detective glanced briefly up to the alcove
before her concentration returned to the match, killing her
next shot into the right-front court corner where the ball
bounced off and then rolled on the court floor, "dead."
A couple of minutes later Huber had caught up, and the
score stayed at 13 points all for a long time, with each
player not wanting to give up the fight and getting the
serve back time after time. Her rival knew that she was
fast on her feet and preferred a game low to the ground.
So to tire her out, he landed a few well-placed ceiling shots,
which Huber returned, but they left her at a disadvantage.
Finally, the man took the last two points by force, hitting
the ball so hard that Huber could not see, let alone hit it in
time. Both players were drenched in sweat and breathing
hard as they shook hands, then took off their protective
goggles and walked out to the hallway where they stowed
racquets, ball, gloves and goggles in their bags.

Moments later, Andi found her boss outside the court
door stretched out on her back with a towel tucked under
her head. She was rotating her knees, pulling each up to
her waist in turn. Her opponent had already left.

Andi asked, "You okay, Mrs. Huber?"

"Certainly! I need to do warm-up and cool-down exercises before and after each match, otherwise these old bones of mine will cave in."

"They seem to be holdin' up damn good! You ran circles around that guy, and the only reason he won is because he overpowered you in the end."

Huber laughed and said, "That's allowed, you know."

"What is?"

"Using power is part of the game."

"Yeah, but he really turned it on. I mean, he's younger and a man."

Huber was now doing leg-stretches and said, "Well dear, I've learned a life-time ago that when competing with the boys, we play on their terms!"

"Reckon that's true," Andi admitted.

They fell silent while Huber finished her exercise routine. She looked up at Andi and decided that the young woman from New Orleans had not changed much since bursting into her office looking for work over two years earlier. The auburn hair was falling around her shoulders in a mass of unruly waves as always, framing her porcelain complexion and mischievous cat-like green eyes. She was clad in jeans, a black leather jacket and cowboy boots, and the helmet she carried under her arm indicated that, as usual, she had ridden over on her Harley-Davidson.

Andi gazed down at her boss sprawled on the floor, red-faced from exertion, wearing running shorts, a tee shirt and high-top athletic shoes. Mrs. Huber's appearance was in contrast with her customary chic elegance. I guess she's in her sixties, she thought. What a jock! And a good thing she quit smoking too.

Finished with her cool-down, Huber said, "Surely you didn't come here just to watch me play. So what's up?"

"Well, ma'am, I'm afraid murder might be."

Astonished, her boss asked, "You've got a murder case for us to solve?"

Andi grimaced and admitted, "Actually, only a missing person, but I betcha she's gotten herself killed."

# Chapter 2

Later that morning the two gathered in R. A. Huber's office on North Lake Avenue in Pasadena. The Swiss-born seasoned private investigator and the dynamic young woman from the Deep South made an excellent team. Not once in the last two and a half years did Huber ever regret having hired the fiery redhead. What the novice lacked in experience she made up in ingenuity.

Andi eyed the Staunton Rosewood chessboard with the chessmen set up at one end of Huber's desk and said, "Wish I knew how to play."

"I'll teach you on a rainy day," her boss replied.

The young woman gently picked up one of the knights and, studying it, remarked, "Top quality craftsmanship. Is it a valuable antique?"

"I have no idea about its monetary worth, but the set is of sentimental value to me as it belonged to my father."

"I know watcha mean. I cherish Daddy's old helmet, dents and all."

Then Huber said, "Now let's get down to business. Tell me about your missing person."

"Her name is Elena Campione and she's my friend."

"How did you meet?"

"We have some classes together."

"So she is a kid about your age, then?"

Andi raised both eyebrows and replied, "Elena is a little older than me and married. Not exactly a toddler, I'd think."

"Sorry, dear, I'll take that back. You are both young women, of course! Now fill me in about your friend's disappearance."

"Okay. Elena had played hooky at school for a couple of days, but I didn't think anything of it as she'd done that before. She was supposed to have dinner with me at Mario's on October 9 - - that was a Thursday - - while her husband was out of town, but she stood me up. I called her house later that night, but nobody answered. Then I phoned her again after she still hadn't shown up at school and only got her machine, just like before. At that point I was pissed and figured that she must've decided at the last minute to go along to Arizona with her husband, forgetting about our dinner plans."

She continued, "It wasn't until over a week later that I started to worry about her. She hadn't returned to class and I remembered that she told me her husband would be on his business trip for about a week. More days went by without seeing or hearing from her, so yesterday, I finally called to find out if she was sick or something. I talked with her husband and learned that she has disappeared and is reported missing. The police traced her to Albuquerque, but there the trail ends."

"I see."

"No you don't, ma'am!" Andi burst out. "The man is beside himself with worry and so am I. Of course I didn't let on that I expect the worst, but I told him about you, Mrs. Huber, and that I'm your part-time assistant. I said that we could find Elena for him, so he wants to hire us."

"You had better tell me all you know, then."

Andi reached into her jeans pocket and, pulling out a piece of paper, said, "Reckoned you'd want to know the dates so I wrote them all down. Let me see - - Bruno Campione told me that he came back from Arizona Monday evenin', October 13 and found a note from Elena at their house. The note said something like 'Need to get away for a while, don't bother looking for me.' He said he'd called her on her cell phone on Friday and she'd told him she was out and about, running errands. The note wasn't dated, so when he read it on that Monday he figured she had gone somewhere for the weekend and would come home at any moment. By the next day he checked with some of her friends and relatives, but no one had seen her. Her car was gone and so were a good-sized bag and her make-up case. At that point he got worried and called the police to report her missing."

She went on, "The police put out an APB for her car and it was found in the parking lot of a hotel in Albuquerque. She'd checked into the hotel on Thursday, October 9 and had apparently planned to stay five days, paying cash for the room in advance. She was seen walking to the bus parking lot where the shuttle took her to the Balloon Fiesta Park every mornin' for the last three days of the festival. Her room had evidently not been disturbed or the bed slept in from Sunday to Monday, or the next night. The hotel manager called the Albuquerque authorities on Tuesday afternoon when her car was still parked in the hotel lot. By that time our own police force was already looking for Elena's BMW."

Andi shook her head sadly and said, "So there you have it. Nobody has seen her since Sunday mornin', October 12, when she took the bus headed for the balloon field."

They both kept silent for a long time. Huber was mulling the story over in her mind while absent mindedly fingering the black queen on her chess board.

She remarked, "The young woman hasn't been missing for all that long, you know."

Andi replied, "She got to Albuquerque October 9, the day we were supposed to have dinner together, and I'd think that it took her at least two days to drive there, so I reckon she left home on October 7 and today is the 21st. That's two weeks for crying out loud!"

"You forget that she was last seen in Albuquerque on the 12th, so she has only been missing for nine days."

"Guess you're right."

Then Huber asked, "Has it occurred to you that Elena may have wanted to disappear?"

"Why would her car still be at the hotel, then?"

"She could have had a rendezvous with someone at the festival and taken off with that person."

Andi looked skeptical but didn't contradict her boss.

After a pause Huber inquired, "How well do you know Elena?"

"She's one of the few friends I've made at college and I see her occasionally outside of school."

"Describe her to me."

"Pretty, blonde, blue-eyed, with a dancer's body. She has a sweet disposition but is rather immature."

"Do you know anything about her background?"

"A little. She told me that she hardly ever sees her parents as they disapprove of her. She dropped out of college in her sophomore year. Then she worked as a waitress for a few months until she applied for a job as a dancer at Bruno Campione's club and ended up marrying him." Andi smiled and added, "She seems happy enough in her marriage as far as I can tell.

"I told her a little about my growin' up in New Orleans and that Daddy is dead, and she shared how she'd adored her grandmother who had also passed away. She'll soon inherit a fortune from that grandmother when turning 25, by the way."

"Does she have any siblings?"

Andi took a moment to think and then answered, "I don't think she ever mentioned any."

Huber remarked, "Looks like she decided to get an education after all since she is your classmate at Pasadena City College."

"Yeah, her husband urged her to go back to school."

"Good for him! What kind of impression did you get of the young man? I assume he *is* young?"

"We haven't met in person. I just talked to him on the phone."

"Did you say that he owns a nightclub?"

"That's right, The Gem in Pasadena."

"The Gem! I'm impressed. The establishment is not your average, sleazy nightclub. It has class."

Surprised, Andi asked, "You've been inside?"

Huber nodded and said, "My son and daughter were in town for one of my bigger birthdays and gave me a unique present. I love to dance, so they arranged for babysitting for their kids and took us to The Gem." And with a chuckle she went on, "Peter and I were by far the oldest couple on the dance floor, but we enjoyed ourselves thoroughly nonetheless!"

Then she said, "You mentioned that Mr. Campione went on a trip to Arizona. Did Elena tell you what that was about?"

"Yeah, he opened another club there and has been spending his time going back and forth between the two businesses lately."

"What do you think about the note she left for him?"

Andi replied, "Doesn't tell us much, does it?"

"I find it interesting!"

The redhead gave her boss a questioning look, but Huber didn't comment further. Andi was scrutinizing her own notes to make sure she had not left any crucial information out. Yes, she thought, I told all I know.

The private investigator, for her part, was reflecting on all she had just learned. She was startled and almost jumped when Andi suddenly burst out, "So Mrs. Huber, are we taking the case?"

"You've got me intrigued; the answer is yes."

"Oh, thank you, ma'am!" Then she looked at her watch and exclaimed, "Shit, I'm late for class!" As she bolted out the door, she said, "Oops, I wasn't going to say that word no more."

Seconds later, Huber heard the familiar roar of the Harley-Davidson as Andi raced out of the parking lot.

# Chapter 3

As Bruno Campione entered R. A. Huber's office for his consultation appointment the next day, his first thought was; an old woman and a wild-looking kid! How could they possibly succeed in finding Elena when so far the police, with all their resources, had failed?

Introductions made, Huber pointed to the client chair and said, "Have a seat, Mr. Campione." And, as if reading his mind, she continued, "Have you heard anything more from the police since Andi talked with you?"

He shook his head and replied, "Not a word."

Huber looked him over. He was tall, about 6'3" she judged, and had classic Roman looks. The nose sat long and narrow over a generous mouth. His eyes were dark brown and so was the short hair which had been recently cut. He was impeccably dressed in a button-down shirt and sports jacket. There was no sign of neglect in his appearance, but there were prominent dark circles under his eyes, suggesting sleepless nights.

It took but a few seconds for her to make these observations and then she said, "Andi filled me in, but I have more questions."

"Go ahead."

She smiled and said, "First off, I want to congratulate you on the success of The Gem!"

"Thank you."

"That is an accomplishment for someone as young as you are, I would say."

As he answered, "I'm 37, not exactly a kid any longer," he appreciated the clever way that Huber had ferreted out his age.

She continued, "You are extremely lucky to own such a business at a top notch location in Old Town Pasadena."

"That's true. Luck has a lot to do with it. My father owned a bar on that lot way before the neighborhood became fashionable. He had purchased the building as well. Some years ago he moved back to Italy to retire and left me with the bar. I was an accountant at the time, working for someone else, but I had always dreamed of having my own business. And again I was lucky when the banker believed in my venture and granted me a loan to remodel and enlarge the place."

Huber beamed at him and remarked, "A colossal endeavor and well done!"

Then she said, "Now to some personal questions. How long have you been married to Elena?"

"Two and a half years."

"Where do her folks live?"

"Prescott, Arizona."

"Andi told me that you opened a club in Arizona. Is it also located in Prescott?"

"No, the club is in Kingman."

"When did the new place open?"

"A few months ago, but there are lots of things left to do before it will eventually run smoothly. That is why I travel back and forth to Kingman so often."

"How did that come about?"

"I don't understand what you mean."

"What made you decide to start another night club in Arizona?"

He took some time before he answered. The truth of the matter was that The Gem was making tons of money and he needed a tax write-off. He was not about to tell that to the woman, though. He drew the line at disclosure when it came to his finances.

He said, "Isn't that the American way?"

"Certainly," she replied, "but why Kingman?"

"Oh, I see your point now. I had been thinking of opening another club somewhere in Nevada at first. Naturally, anywhere near Vegas was out of the question and even Laughlin proved too expensive. The property I happened to find in Kingman was convenient. Land is cheap out there and the building was already standing. It had been a honky tonk bar and dancing, so with some remodeling and renovating, the place was easily converted to a club of my liking."

Suddenly, Huber turned to Andi and said, "Feel free to ask your own questions at any time."

The young woman was jolted out of her reverie and literally jumped. She had been quietly sitting at the edge of Huber's desk, never taking her eyes off Bruno Campione since he had walked into the office. Not in her entire life had she seen such a handsome guy. Now, guilt stricken, she pulled herself together and thought, what's the matter with me? My friend is missing and I make big eyes at her husband.

Aloud she said, "Can't think of anything to ask off hand."

Huber addressed Campione again and inquired, "When did you leave your house on your latest business trip to Kingman?"

"Early Tuesday morning, October 7," he replied.

"Was Elena in good spirits that morning?"

"I didn't talk to her; she was still asleep when I took off."

"I understand that you had a phone conversation with your wife as late as Friday before she disappeared from Albuquerque. Let's see" - - she glanced at her notes - - "that would be Friday, October 10."

"That's right. She said that she was in her car running errands. I took her at face value and naturally thought that she was in the L.A. area. Now I know that she must have already been in New Mexico at the time."

"Did you make any more calls to your wife while away on that business trip?"

"No, but on Sunday evening I called home and left a message on the answering machine telling her that I was wrapping things up in Kingman and planned to be home by Monday night."

"It did not worry you that she failed to pick up?"

"No, I'd assumed she had gone out for the evening."

After a pause Huber said, "The note she left and the fact that she did not tell you her whereabouts when you talked with her on that Friday indicate that she wanted to keep her mission in Albuquerque, whatever that may have been, a secret from you. Have you any idea as to why?"

There was a hopeless look in his eyes when he replied, "I've been racking my brains trying to figure out why she left, but cannot come up with anything reasonable."

"Did you quarrel?"

He seemed vexed at first, then averted his eyes and admitted, "We had a fight the night before I left for Kingman. It was about something stupid and I won't even go into it. At any rate, neither one of us talked about it when I called her on that Friday. Obviously, we had both forgotten about the squabble by then."

"I understand that you contacted Elena's friends and relatives after you discovered her missing, but think hard now, is there anyone that she is close to and may have confided in?"

He took his time and then shook his head and answered, "I can't think of anybody else other than the people I already talked to. I even phoned her former boyfriend; I was that desperate. Calling Ted Wilson, her father, was a real effort for me as the man hates my guts."

Andi found her voice and said, "Mrs. Huber wanted to know if Elena had any siblings, but I didn't know. Does she?"

"Yes. Her sister Brenda is currently a student at Arizona State in Phoenix and her brother Kevin still lives with his parents. They are actually half-brother and half-sister. Elena is the daughter from Ted Wilson's first marriage."

Andi was on a roll now and continued, "Elena told me that she is estranged from her parents. Do you know why?"

"There were issues ever since her teens. Ted Wilson is one of those brilliant people who demand perfection from their family members. Elena couldn't live up to his standards. She never got along with her stepmother either. Marrying me did not help matters. They were appalled that Elena chose a night club owner."

The hurt in his tone of voice was evident when he added, "Ted and Marcia Wilson refused to come to our wedding. The only person who attended from Elena's side of the family was her sister."

"What about her own mother?" Andi wanted to know.

"Oh, her mom died a long time ago when Elena was little. She hardly remembers her."

Then Huber asked, "What are Ted and Marcia Wilson's professions?"

"He is a physicist and she's an attorney."

After a pause the private eye said, "That's all for the moment. I'll need names and addresses, if you have them. You can either e-mail or fax them to me."

"What names and addresses?"

"I'll give you a list in a minute. First I'll tell you what my approximate game plan is." And she elaborated, "I'll talk with people in Prescott and Kingman and take a trip to Albuquerque. I don't know in which order yet. Oh, and I also would like to have a recent picture of your wife. Andi doesn't get a break from school until December, so she will not join me on the trips, but she can work on the case here and be at your disposal between classes.

"As for fee and expenses, I'll prepare an estimate for you."

He exploded, "I don't care about the cost, I just want Elena found!"

Huber had been writing on her yellow pad while talking, and now she handed him the following list, saying, "I need names, phone numbers and addresses, if you have them."

1. Elena's parents
2. Person in charge of Kingman club
3. Hotel in Albuquerque and name of manager
4. Elena's ex boyfriend

He glanced at the list and murmured, "Wilson info - no problem; I know Rocky's number and address by heart, of course; the police gave me the Albuquerque data." When he got to item number four he looked up and asked, "Is it really necessary that you get in touch with her ex boyfriend? He already told me that he hasn't seen her recently."

"He might be more inclined to talk to Andi or me than he would to her husband," Huber put in.

Bruno Campione shrugged and replied, "Perhaps," and the consultation meeting drew to an end.

# Chapter 4

After dinner, Peter and Regula Huber relaxed in the living room of their home in Merida, situated at the foot of the Angeles National Forest Mountains in the San Fernando Valley. The pair, now married for over forty years, sat in their respective recliners in agreeable silence. Peter's full head of white hair was bent over a chapter of his latest manuscript. Every so often, his hazel eyes squinted in concentration, and his generous mustache twitched when he murmured a sentence to himself, as if trying it out for effect. If satisfied, he would nod, and if not, he would pencil in a change onto the printout.

Regula glanced at him and thought, we've grown old together and generally it was an enjoyable ride. There had been hectic times, especially during their kids' teen years, but overall, life had been good to them. She continued her musing, appreciating the fact that Peter was fulfilled with his writing. Some of her friends' husbands had no clue of what to do with themselves after retirement.

Peter suddenly looked up and said, "What are you grinning about?"

"Oh, I was just thanking God that you found such a wonderful hobby."

"What hobby? I take my writing seriously, I'll have you know!"

"Of course you do, and I don't begrudge you your success," she replied with a smile.

"You're living your dream too, Regula. How would you like it if I called your detective business a hobby?"

"Touché!" Then she said, "Andi brought an interesting case our way today."

"Tell me about it."

"Sure you want me to? I would hate to interrupt your train of thought."

"I can go back to my proofreading later, so shoot."

"All right, then," she said, and related all she knew about the disappearance of Elena to him.

When she had finished, Peter chuckled and said, "If I'd want to vanish, I'd pick the launch field at the Albuquerque balloon festival too! And in case she was abducted, I can't think of a better place and time to snatch someone away while thousands of spectators are staring into the sky, not paying any attention of what goes on at ground level."

"You hit the nail on the head," his spouse remarked.

Then he said, "That Bruno fellow owns The Gem. How impressive! What did you think of the man?"

"I liked him."

"Do you have a plan of how to proceed?"

"Vaguely. I'll tend to the out-of-town part of the investigation, while Andi will pry into matters close by. That reminds me, I had better tell Andi to find out if the Campiones have a housekeeper. I forgot to ask Bruno Campione today."

She continued, "I think I'll drive to Prescott first as I'm real curious about Elena's folks. Then I may stop in Kingman where Bruno Campione's new club is located before I start the long journey to Albuquerque. Want to come along?"

Peter said, "I can't possibly be in Arizona and New Mexico when I'm traveling up and down the state of California."

"Oh, I totally forgot about your book-signing tour! You're leaving Friday, right?"

"Definitely! That's the day after tomorrow."

"I was hoping to combine a little pleasure with work, but I guess I'll have to brave the trip by myself."

# Chapter 5

On Thursday, R. A. Huber took care of household chores, made phone calls to the Wilson residence in Prescott and to Rocky Santoro in Kingman scheduling meetings with them, and also had a short conference with Andi. In the evening, she helped Peter decide on the wardrobe he needed to pack for his tour. He was going to be gone for nearly two weeks and wanted only to take a medium-sized suitcase. Miraculously, his wife found room for all his items, including a suit and dress shoes, and was even able to close the zipper. Then she quickly packed her own bag.

Early Friday morning, the couple locked up their house, kissed good-bye, and drove off in opposite directions. Peter headed north-west, where his tour would lead him along the California coast, and Regula started on her journey due east.

About an hour into her drive, turning away from the 210 freeway, the lady detective braced herself for the long and boring stretch ahead on Interstate 10. She inserted a disc from Queen and while listening to the music let her thoughts run wild. Soon she was dwelling on her current case, thinking, the longer Elena remains missing, the more Andi's suspicion of kidnapping and foul play makes sense. On the other hand, she reflected, it was possible that the young woman had wanted to disappear without a trace. Leaving her car in the hotel parking lot may have been part of the vanishing act. There were plenty of avenues open to Elena if she had wanted to leave of her own free will. For instance, going south from Albuquerque on Interstate 25 would take her straight to the Mexican border at El Paso. She could have accomplished this with someone's help, or taken public transportation.

Huber wished that she knew more about Elena's personality and hoped that the woman's parents would be willing to tell her a great deal. Was she too optimistic in assuming that they would open up to her when meeting face to face? Ted Wilson had sounded less than enthusiastic on the phone, but in the end had agreed to see her. Come to think of it, he had not seemed particularly alarmed that his daughter was missing.

The Palm Springs turn-off was coming up in the next mile, and Huber contemplated briefly if she was going to allow herself the little detour and have lunch there. She checked the time; it was only 10:30. As she drove by the exit, she looked in the direction of the windmills with longing but kept going. *I'll stop in Blythe for lunch*, she decided.

When she was back on the road after her break, traffic slowed to a crawl for many miles due to road construction. By the time she left Interstate 10 and merged onto US-60 E, it was already late in the afternoon. She soon passed a road marker: 120 miles to Prescott. *With any luck, I'll get there before dark*, she thought. Along Highway 71 she spotted signs pointing out ghost towns nearby. Then she entered AZ-89 N for the end leg of her journey. The last stretch was extremely curvy and she was bone tired as she reached the town of Prescott.

She turned into Gurley Street and stopped for the night at a hotel close to Hassayampa, an upscale area of Prescott where Ted and Marcia Wilson lived.

# Chapter 6

Ted Wilson peered at his wife from behind the newspaper and sighed. The two sat at the breakfast nook in the spacious kitchen of their home.

Marcia asked, "What's wrong?"

He replied, "What on earth was I thinking when I agreed to see that private investigator woman?"

"You're having regrets already?"

"There's nothing we can tell her, so it's a waste of time for all concerned."

His spouse looked at him with amusement and said, "Admit it; you just can't stand being kept away from your lab. As for me, I can think of lots of ways I'd rather spend my Saturday morning. But Ted, you really had no choice. We have to talk to her."

"I don't see why."

"She'd assume we had something to hide if we'd refused to see her."

"As usual, you're thinking with your lawyer mind. The way I look at it, we've already talked with the police and we don't owe this Mrs. Huber a thing."

"No, but maybe she'll find Elena."

"I doubt it," her husband replied.

He was 51 and Marcia's senior by six years. She studied him briefly. He could be stubborn at times, but she admired most of his qualities. The fact that he appeared like an absent-minded professor, not caring how he dressed or what he looked like, was especially endearing. He was of average looks with a height of 5'10" and medium build, light-brown hair and gray eyes, but there was nothing average about his brain, she thought. His mind was brilliant.

She asked, "Can you put the money back into Elena's fund before she turns 25?"

"You know well enough that things haven't turned out as planned."

"I'm aware of that, but the bottom line is, *can you raise the money before her birthday?*"

Sighing again, he replied, "Believe me, I'm trying my damndest, but I may not make the deadline." He could not hide the anger in his voice as he continued, "It's all Mother's fault. What right did she have cheating me out of my inheritance? Being eccentric is one thing, but leaving her fortune to Elena on a whim was downright irresponsible. They are two of a kind, neither having any idea of what's important in life." And he shouted, "What the hell is Elena going to do with her millions anyhow? Open a dance studio?"

As fast as Ted's temper had flared up, it faded away just as quickly and he silently bent his head back over the paper he was reading.

Marcia was left to her own pondering as she drank the last few sips of her morning coffee. She wished that Ted was less of a fanatic when it came to his research. If she'd let him, he'd spend all of their money down to the last penny on equipment, materials and items needed for his studies. Granted, he had made some earthshaking discoveries and his efforts were certainly worth the trouble and time he took to arrive at his findings. All had been well and good while the government financed his projects, but when federal budget cuts were made, the funding for Ted's research had come to a halt. He was contracting for the private sector now, but a good portion of the money for his undertakings came out of his own pocket. He hadn't consulted her when "borrowing" from Elena's trust, or she would have strongly advised against it. She had only learned about his fingers in Elena's pot when he was unable to replace the funds.

Marcia was jolted back to the present as her husband abruptly got up from his stool and said, "I'm going to the lab until the woman gets here."

She looked up at the kitchen clock and replied, "Mrs. Huber's appointment is at ten o'clock. That's in half an hour, so don't get too carried away!" And as he passed her on his way to the door she added, "I'd change sweaters before she comes, if I were you."

Ted glanced at his favorite, well-worn cardigan and said, "There's nothing wrong with this one; it's comfortable."

# Chapter 7

The private investigator arrived at 10:00 a.m. sharp and parked her Buick on the circular driveway of the opulent Tuscan home. She walked along the path made of paving stones to the main entrance, surveying the perfectly landscaped front yard of shrubs, cactus plants and potted flowers before ringing the bell.

Marcia Wilson opened the door and said, ushering her in, "The family room is probably most convenient."

Huber followed her out of a vaulted ceiling entrance hall and, as she did, got a glimpse of the formal living and dining rooms when they passed by the open doors. An air of simple elegance was evident throughout the house, and the family room was no exception.

Marcia motioned her to the sofa group and said, "Have a seat. Would you like anything to drink?"

"Thanks for the offer, but I just had breakfast."

"I'll go get my husband, then. He's working in his research laboratory."

Left alone, Huber looked the room over. The top quality furniture, polished hardwood floor and sculptured fire place left her with an overall impression of soigné good taste. All that was lacking was warmth, she mused. She had had the same image concerning the lady of the house. Marcia radiated "chic smart" in her sleek leisure slacks and sequined blouse. Tall, slim with dark hair, the woman was attractive in a well-groomed manner, but the stare of her brown eyes was impersonal and cold.

Huber was just about to get up from the couch to examine a print on the far wall, when a teenager stuck his head in and said, "Oh, sorry!"

He had already disappeared from view when she called him back, saying, "You must be Kevin."

He nodded. "And who are you?"

"My name is R. A. Huber."

He took a step into the room and blurted, "You're kidding! The sleuth who's looking for Elena?"

"So you know about me."

"Mom told me, but - -" he broke off and stared at the lady detective.

"You expected someone younger," Huber said with amusement.

"Yeah, a lot younger and bigger," he admitted with a child's honesty.

Huber smiled and tapping her forehead said, "Sometimes brain work is more important than muscle in my job." Then she asked, "How old are you, Kevin?"

"15."

"A high school sophomore, I take it?"

"No, a senior, I skipped a couple of years."

"Ah, a smarty! Do you know where you're headed after you graduate?"

"Yep, I'll start at ERAU."

"What is ERAU?"

"Embry-Riddle Aeronautical University," he replied.

"So you're interested in a career in aviation. Good for you. Is the campus far away?"

He grinned and said, "ERAU is right here in Prescott. Their curriculum covers engineering, research, manufacturing, marketing and management of modern aircraft, but what I'm most interested in is the aerospace program."

There was undisguised excitement in Kevin's voice as he uttered that last sentence, and his eagerness about attending the university was evident.

"You can hardly wait, right?"

"You got it!"

Then she said, "Now tell me about Elena."

"I have no idea where she is."

"Of course not, or you'd have come forward with that info a long time ago."

He nodded.

"Just tell me about your sister. For instance, what is she like? Do you get along? What do you have in common? Things like that."

He thought for a second and then answered, "She's an airhead and thinks that I'm a nerd. We didn't exactly fight but stayed away from each other. The only thing we have in common is the same father."

They heard the back door being opened and a moment later Kevin's parents entered the room.

Ted Wilson stretched out his hand and said, "Sorry for the wait, Mrs. Huber." Then glancing at his son, he added, "I see you found someone to pass the time with."

Huber did a quick study of the man. He looked sloppy next to his immaculate wife, but the eyes that met hers gleamed with intelligence. The boy had inherited his mother's complexion and dark hair, but clearly his father's eyes.

Marcia Wilson sat down on the sofa next to Huber while her husband chose a chair facing the two women.

Kevin stayed standing, not sure what was expected of him, and then murmured, "I've got stuff to do," nodded to Huber and left.

# Chapter 8

Huber said, "Your home is lovely."

"Thanks," Ted Wilson replied. "The main reason we bought this particular property is because it has a detached guest home which I converted into a lab."

"I saw the structure from the street and was wondering if it housed domestic staff."

"We're not that fancy. We only have a housekeeper who comes" - - he turned to his spouse - - "how often?"

"Once a week," Marcia put in.

Huber asked, "You are a scientist, correct?"

"A physicist, to be exact."

"I don't know what a physicist does," she admitted.

"Lots of people don't. Let me tell you in a few words what the job entails."

Marcia thought, oh no! Let's hope he keeps it at *a few words*. This could take all day.

"In general, physicists analyze various forms of energy, the structure and physical properties of matter, and the relationship between the two. Our research and findings often result in new technologies. Without physicists, mankind would not have radar, television, x-ray machines, lasers, atomic power, and more.

"There are theoretical physicists who work with mathematical formulas and experimental physicists who use systematic observation and measurement. I do both, depending on what I'm working on, and sometimes design new instruments for the purpose of my studies. This may sound like a tedious and boring job to you, but I find it fascinating. Naturally, there are also frustrations as projects can fail and all the time and money put into them seems wasted.

"A good portion of physicists with Ph.D.'s teach and lecture at universities." With a smirk he added, "I'm afraid that I lack the patience for a teaching position."

She asked, "You are self-employed, then?"

"Now I am, but I used to work for the government for many years. I set up my own research laboratory soon after we moved here."

"How long ago was that?"

Marcia replied, "Six years," before he had time to answer.

He looked at his wife and said, "I guess you're right. It doesn't seem that long to me, though."

Huber smiled and said, "So how's business?"

"Not too many profitable jobs have come my way, lately. There is a plus side to that; I can work on whatever I want in between clients."

"I don't understand."

"What I mean is, when I get hired as a contractor to perform research for a certain project, the paying client, whether a company from the private sector or a government agency, calls the shots. Whereas when I'm out of work, I can research any project my heart desires."

"Who finances your recreational ventures?"

He chuckled and replied, "You're sharp! Marcia, as a partner in a law firm, is able to support my between-jobs habit." And he went on, "At the moment I'm completely absorbed in the research of - -"

His wife interrupted, "I think that's enough shop talk. I'm sure Mrs. Huber wants to get to the reason she came to see us."

He said, "Oh yes, I almost forgot that you wanted to talk about Elena."

Astonished at his carefree tone of voice, Huber asked, "You're not concerned about your daughter's disappearance?"

"Not in the least. She'll turn up when she's ready. Running away when things don't go according to her wishes has always been Elena's style. She was seven when she ran away from home for the first time. Granted, it wasn't far. We lived in Phoenix at the time and her grandmother's house was only a few blocks away."

"When was the last time you saw her?"

"I think it was last December, a few days before Christmas."

"That's almost a year ago. Am I correct in assuming that your relationship with Elena is strained?"

"I hate to admit it, but that's true. The problems go back a long way, but she really blew it when she dropped out of college in her sophomore year. Elena defied me in many other ways too, and she never saw eye to eye with her stepmother."

Annoyed, Marcia thought, he surely is warming up to this woman in a hurry. An hour ago, he was reluctant to talk to her and now he's giving out all sorts of personal info.

She gave him a reproachful stare and then turned to the private eye and stated, "Elena was not an easy child to deal with and her teenage years were less than satisfactory. Not being her actual mother, I tried hard to win her over, but she refused to give me a chance at parenting."

"Yes, that can be difficult." Then she turned back to the man and asked, "Mr. Wilson, what is your issue with Elena now that she is an adult?"

He paused before replying, as if he had to think this over, and then said, "I was extremely angry at her when she called one day out of the blue and informed me that she had left school and Phoenix for good. She had not deemed it necessary to tell us of her plan in advance. No, she phoned after the fact letting me know that she was staying with a friend in the Los Angeles area and that she was working as a waitress."

He continued, "After that, we didn't hear from her for many months and when she finally called again it was to present us with yet another bombshell. This time she announced that she was getting married."

"I take it that you were not pleased with the news," Huber remarked.

He shook his head in disgust and said, "You've got that right. The man owns a nightclub, for Pete's sake! And with a name like Bruno Campione, he may be connected to the mob, for all I know."

"We have no proof of that," his spouse interjected.

"Must you always speak in lawyer's terms?" he shot back at her.

"My dear Ted, you really need to be more careful of what you accuse people of."

Huber took this opportunity and asked, "Are you a defense lawyer or do you work for the prosecution?"

"Neither, I'm a corporate attorney," she replied.

Getting back to Elena, don't you think that it's possible that she was abducted in Albuquerque?"

"Rubbish!" her father declared. "Why would she drive there to begin with, all by herself, if she wasn't running away?"

"Maybe she simply needed some time alone and decided on the balloon festivities in New Mexico."

"Without letting anyone know what she was up to? No, I don't buy it!"

"Don't forget, Mr. Wilson, she is no longer a child rebelling against authority. She is a young and, from what I understand, happily married woman. So why do you think she ran away?"

"She may have gotten in a fight with that husband of hers. As I already told you, Elena has a habit of running from things rather than facing them. Or she is already tired of the man and ran away with another. Who knows?"

"You think that's likely?"

"I haven't seen much of her in the last few years, so she may be a different person now, but in her senior year of high school, the girl changed boyfriends like shirts instead of paying attention to her studies."

"When is her 25th birthday?"

"November 7, why do you ask?"

"I heard that she will come into an inheritance at that time."

He seemed irate as he answered, "Campione surely is a blabbermouth! Yes, he told you the truth; Elena will come into most of my mother's fortune when turning 25. Until then, the money is invested and I'm holding it in a trust for her."

"That is rather unusual, isn't it?"

"What is?"

"That the lady left her money to her granddaughter, skipping a generation, so to speak."

"Yes, Mother was an eccentric, but that is hardly any of your business."

"Sorry, I didn't mean to pry. By the way, I learned about Elena's trust from my assistant, who is a friend of your daughter, not from Mr. Campione," and she briefly explained that Andi and Elena were taking classes together at PCC.

Surprised, he queried, "Elena is back in school?"

Huber nodded.

"She must be taking dance or drama or the like."

"As far as I know, she is enrolled in standard classes working toward her BA."

"Out of her own free will?  Amazing!"

"I believe that her husband suggested it."

"I give him credit for that.  Perhaps the man isn't as bad as I thought."

Huber said, "So neither one of you has heard from Elena recently?"

They shook their heads in unison.

"This is just a formality, but do you remember where you were on Sunday, October 12?"

Marcia replied, "I'm afraid we do not have any proper alibis.  Ted was home all day doing research, and I ran some errands around town, none of which we can prove. On that evening, we attended a dinner party, which we *can* prove."

Then Huber said, "I won't intrude on you any longer. Thank you for giving up some of your valuable time to talk to me."  And getting up from the sofa she added, "Oh, just one more thing.  I understand you have another daughter who is currently away at college?"

"That's right.  Brenda is attending Arizona State University in Phoenix and is doing an excellent job academically."

"May I have her phone number, please?"

"I doubt that Brenda has a clue of where you'll find Elena, but all right, I'll give it to you."

Equipped with that piece of information, the lady detective left the Wilson household.

# Chapter 9

On that Saturday afternoon Andi was riding her Harley-
Davidson to the famous club in Old Town Pasadena. She
chose to take surface streets from her aunt and uncle's
house where she currently lived. For a brief time the
young woman had enjoyed a place of her own in Century
City, but when starting college, she had moved back to
Pasadena where her relatives owned a house just a few
blocks away from the school and a short ride from R.A.
Huber's office.

When Bruno Campione had suggested meeting at his
place of business, Andi eagerly agreed in anticipation
of getting a glimpse inside The Gem. She had ridden or
walked by the club numerous times and often wondered
what was contained within. Now, heading down Colorado
Boulevard, she made a mental list of questions she'd ask
Elena's husband. Reckon the man is real anxious by now,
she thought. He must realize that with each new day, the
chances of finding Elena alive and well are getting slimmer.
Sure, he'd pulled himself together on Wednesday at Mrs.
Huber's, but the dread and worry showing in his eyes had
been too great to miss.

She turned left into a side street and two blocks down
the road saw the imposing neon sign, THE GEM. She rode
into the alley leading behind the building and parked her
Harley in the lot. Then she took off her helmet, tucking

it under one arm while shaking her abundant auburn hair loose, and walked toward the back entrance of the structure. Getting no response to her vigorous knocking, she tried to open the door. It was locked. Certain that Mr. Campione had instructed her to go to the *back* door, she was about to turn away to search for another rear entry to the place when the door was abruptly flung open by a giant.

Andi let out an involuntary shriek. The mere size of the man was intimidating. She was a tall woman of 5'9" but felt like a child gazing up at him. He was also wide and seemed to fill out the massive doorframe with his bulk. His piercing gray eyes were close-set and his head was shaved.

"Andi?"

"Yes sir."

"I'm Phil Drummer. Come on in. Bruno isn't here yet, but you can wait in his office."

She followed him down a corridor and watched him swing his broad shoulders and arms in perfect rhythm with each step of his droll gait.

Halfway down the hall he stopped and motioned her into a room, saying, "I can offer you coffee, soda, or water. I doubt you're old enough for anything stronger."

Andi had turned 21 two weeks previously, but let it go and just said, "Nothing, thank you."

"My office is next door; holler if you need anything."

Andi was getting used to the man's appearance and was no longer petrified by it. As he made his way out the door she called him back and said, "Just a minute, sir! I reckon you're an employee of Mr. Campione?"

He swung around and replied, "No doubt about it!"

"What is your position?"

"I'm the manager." And grinning, he added, "On occasion I also help out as bouncer."

"I'll bet!" Then she gave him a dazzling smile and said, "I'd be tickled to death to have a look at The Gem!"

"There's nothing going on in there now. The club doesn't open to the public until nighttime." He looked at his watch and stated, "It's even too early for the staff to get here."

"Oh, I figured, but could I just have a quick peek? I'm not a minor, so you wouldn't be breakin' any rules!" She fumbled in the back pocket of her jeans for I.D.

He gave it a brief glance and then said, "Okay, there's no harm in letting you have a look, then." And pointing to the helmet Andi was still clutching to herself, he mockingly added, "You can leave that on the desk here; no one would want to steal it!"

He guided her down the hallway continuing in the same direction they had taken to the office until arriving at double doors which he pushed open. Then he flipped on the lights and, letting her pass said, "I've got some paperwork to finish. Turn off the lights when you're through."

Andi had to get her eyes adjusted to the radiant lighting coming from the ceiling chandeliers as well as the wall fixtures. She took a few steps inside the vast room and then stood immobile, taking it all in.

Immediately to her left sat a bar of enormous size and to her right was the bandstand. Straight in front of her stretched the formidable hardwood dance floor in a huge semicircle. Behind it, small tables and chairs were grouped, also in a circular fashion. Beyond the seating was a reception area leading to the front entrance of the club. The most amazing element was the life-size photographs displayed on all walls. An entire century of popular dances and legendary performers were represented. The gigantic prints were in black and white, which added to their merit of class.

The earliest photograph was of can-can dancers in the Moulin Rouge, Paris. Then came the flappers of the Roaring Twenties doing the Charleston. Next was a print of Radio City Music Hall, New York, with the grandeur of the Rockettes in a chorus line of precision dance. Legends Fred Astaire and Ginger Rogers in the 1935 movie *Top Hat* were depicted, as well as ballroom swing dancers in the big band era of the '40s and '50s. The famous scene from the 1952 movie *Singing in the Rain* with Gene Kelly dancing in street puddles adorned the wall, as did Juliet Prowse performing a Latin number in Las Vegas. Next came night club scenes from all over the country showing crowded dance floors with dancers in bell bottoms doing the Twist in the '60s, the disco era in the '70s when wearing polyester was the mode, and funky style dancers in parachute pants in the '80s. Salsa dancing during the '90s all the way to the present days of hip hop was also immortalized.

Andi walked over to the life-sized pictures, admiring each one in turn. She stood in front of Juliet Prowse's portrait for a long time studying the long, slender, well-formed leg extended in a high kick and then exclaimed, "I don't know who you are, lady, but you've got style!"

Then she took long strides to the center of the dance floor, aware of her reflection bouncing off the mirror-shine on the hardwood ballroom flooring. She glanced over to the bandstand and pictured Daddy standing there, gliding the bow over the strings of his fiddle tucked between shoulder and neck. She imagined him playing her favorite Cajun waltz, moving his head in harmony with the tempo. He seemed so real all of a sudden, nodding at her, a twinkle in his eye. She could actually hear the music in her mind and tapped her cowboy boot to the beat. Before long, she started swaying to the tune and then waltzing away, twirling and twirling, making full use of the entire dance floor.

"What the hell do you think you're doing?"

Andi stopped dead in her tracks and looked in the direction of the familiar voice. An agitated Bruno Campione stood at the back door.

# Chapter 10

Moments later, they were facing one another in his office. Something close to despair was showing in the man's face, which filled Andi with empathy. She thought; how could I've been making a carefree fool of myself while his wife and my friend may have come to harm? He must think me an insensitive, cold-blooded bitch!

She said, "I'm awfully sorry! I don't know what came over me out there on the dance floor."

"Forget it."

"That was unprofessional of me. Elena is a dancer!"

"Forget it, I tell you!" he shot back.

There followed an awkward silence.

Then he said, "I heard from the police."

Andi's pulse quickened and she asked, "They found Elena?"

"No, but here are the damning facts: Her passport is still in her bureau drawer at home, so chances are nil that she flew out of the country. The lieutenant assured me that nowadays, getting a fake passport that'll stand muster is out of the question. He also doubts that she made it into Mexico without proper papers, as sneaking across that border is no easy task any longer. We have to assume that she has not left the United States."

He sighed and went on, "Elena withdrew a total of $1500 from her savings account in increments of $500, the daily limit at ATM machines. The first was here in Pasadena on October 7, the next in Phoenix October 8, and the last in Gallup October 9. There have been no more withdrawals since then. She hasn't charged anything to credit cards so far. Paying cash for the hotel in Albuquerque in advance for five days came to roughly $600 plus tax. Even if she stayed at cheap motels, I'd assume that her cost for lodgings before and after Albuquerque would amount to as much or more. Then there is the expense of gasoline, meals, transportation if she travels no longer by car, et cetera. You do the math."

"She's runnin' out of money."

"Or already has," he replied.

Andi knew only too well what this meant, but tried to be optimistic for his sake and said, "Don't lose heart, Mr. Campione; she may have started off with more money in her pocket than you think."

"Call me Bruno, unless you insist on Ms. - -" he paused - - "I don't even know your last name."

"It's LeJeune, but Andi will do fine."

"Is that really your first name?"

"No, Antoinette is, but I go by Andi."

"Antoinette LeJeune," he murmured, "has a nice ring to it."

"Did Elena ever tell you about me?"

"Only that she befriended an orphan from Louisiana. She seemed fascinated that this friend of hers had traveled across country on her own on a motorcycle at the age of 18 from New Orleans all the way to Los Angeles."

Andi grinned and said, "I never thought of myself as an orphan, but I guess that's what I am."

"Did your parents die in an accident?"

Shaking her head she answered, "I never knew my mother; she died when giving birth to me. Daddy brought me up; it was always just him and me. Liver disease is what killed him at the end of my senior high school year."

He gently said, "I can tell that you were close. You must miss him."

"Sure do. He taught me everything I know."

"For instance?"

"Oh, playing the fiddle and dancing the Cajun waltz, fishing, riding the Harley, loading, shooting and taking care of a gun. Stuff like that."

Amused Bruno remarked, "I can picture all of that!"

Then his expression turned grave again as he stated, "The authorities are done with Elena's BMW and want it off their hands. I spent a good part of today making arrangements for someone to pick it up in New Mexico and drive it home. I don't have the stomach to do it myself."

"I understand."

He seemed lost in thought and then exploded, "I blame myself for what happened."

"How come?"

"Elena is needy and hates that I go out of town so much lately. I shouldn't leave her alone that often; she tends to brood."

"About what?"

"She's never recovered from losing her grandmother, who died when Elena was in college."

"Is that why she quit?"

"I'm sure that was one of the reasons she dropped out, among several." He continued, "She came along to Kingman a few times, but frankly I prefer to go without her."

"Why?"

"Have you been to Kingman?"

"No, sir."

"Bruno, please."

"No, Bruno."

"Well, there isn't much to do there. Elena was bored during the day and wanted to dance all night at the club. I was busy all day and tired at night."

Andi remarked, "I can see your dilemma." Then she asked, "You met her when she applied for a job at The Gem, right?"

A melancholy smile swept over him as he replied, "She walked in asking for an audition. We do offer live entertainment on weekends, but I generally don't hire people off the street. Phil was ready to turn her away, but something about the girl made me feel sorry for her. I'm a pretty good judge of character and could tell that she'd been around the block, but I also saw that she was vulnerable and naïve. So I granted her the audition. To my surprise, she was not just a pretty face but had real talent as a dancer and performer. Her training had been in ballet and jazz, and she did a superb job of choreography by combining the two. I told her to come back after turning 21 and thought that most likely we would not meet again."

He grinned and said, "Two months later, exactly on her birthday, she showed up at The Gem again and I hired her on the spot."

"And then you married her."

"Not on the same day," he replied with a spark of humor. And his eyes took on a faraway stare as he added, "She's emotionally dependent and in many ways helpless. I wanted to guide, protect and take care of her." Then he looked straight at Andi and professed, "I certainly messed up!"

Neither spoke for a while. Bruno thought; why am I telling this untamed kid all this? I must be mad. Andi for her part mused; he looks so crushed and lost. Time to get down to business before we both burst into tears. What happened to the way I had this talk all figured out on the ride over?

So she started her rehearsed speech, "Mrs. Huber called me today and said she'd had an interesting interview with Mr. and Mrs. Wilson. Since there were obviously ill feelings about Elena's inheritance on the part of the Wilsons, my boss didn't want to get into details with them about it. This is a terrible thing to ask you right now, but Mrs. Huber is wondering if you know who'll inherit from Elena."

He stared at her for a second and then replied, "I have no idea."

"She didn't make a will?"

"What do you think? She's 24, for crying out loud, and not even in possession of the money yet!"

"Who'd get her inheritance at this point? Would the money go back to her family or are you next in line?"

He was angry now and shouted, "Just say it: You mean what happens to her trust if she *dies before her 25th birthday!* The answer is, I have no idea, and I don't care. You'd have to ask her estate lawyer."

"That was my next question; do you know who he is?"

"He's in Phoenix and I don't remember the name off hand, but I'll look him up in our address book."

"Thank you! Mrs. Huber is on her way to Kingman now and has an appointment to talk with the man who runs your club there."

"I'm aware of that. I told Rocky to give her his full cooperation."

Then Andi inquired, "Do you have a housekeeper?"

"A cleaning lady comes on Wednesdays. Her name is Celia Molina and I believe the police already questioned her. I'm positive that Elena did not confide in her, but I'll give you her number if you like."

"Please."

"On second thought, I'd better set up the appointment myself, otherwise she may not want to talk to you. Anything else?"

"You already gave us the info about her former boyfriend, David Driscol. I'd best tackle him next."

"I doubt that the little twerp can tell you anything useful, but good luck."

"You've met?"

He nodded. "Only briefly. He came to The Gem one evening soon after Elena and I were married and caused a scene. It was before the club opened, but some of the personnel were already at work. Someone was pounding furiously on the doors and Phil went to check what the racket was about. As soon as he unlocked the entrance, Driscol ran past him demanding to see Elena. When Phil told him that she wasn't there, he made a complete ass of himself, accusing us of keeping her hidden against her will. I was about to leave the office and go home when I heard the commotion and hurried down the corridor to the club. Phil was in the process of physically throwing the guy out, but I stopped him and eventually was able to talk some sense into the loser and he left peacefully."

"What was his problem?"

"Evidently, he was still in love with Elena and had a hard time letting go. It didn't help matters that he was drunk on that particular evening."

Then Andi said, "I just thought of something. You mentioned that Elena withdrew money from several ATM machines on her way to Albuquerque. Tell me again where."

He replied, "Pasadena, Phoenix and Gallup."

"That's what I thought you said.  But why Phoenix?"

"I don't follow you."

"Wouldn't it have made more sense for her to drive to Barstow and take Interstate 40 from there if she was drivin' to Albuquerque?  Why make a detour through Phoenix taking Interstate 10?"

"I didn't realize it, but you're right; it was definitely not the most direct route for her to take."

"You figure she didn't know where she was headed when she took off from home and played her trip by ear?"

"Possibly."  And he added sadly, "Or she didn't want to take the chance of running into me as that stretch of I-40 passes by Kingman.  It always boils down to the same question: *Why did she go on this secretive trip?*"

Realizing that she had touched a sore spot Andi quickly stated, "That's all, then, unless you can think of anyone else I should talk to."

"No, but if somebody comes to mind I'll let you know."

She jumped to her feet and was already at the door when he called out to her "Hey Andi!"

She turned her head and said, "Yes, Bruno?"

"Sorry for snapping at you earlier."

She mimicked him with his own previous words and replied, "Forget it!"

When she had disappeared into the hallway, he couldn't suppress the little smile that showed on his face.

# Chapter 11

Kingman is spread out into three sections spaced somewhat apart: uptown, historic downtown and an unpretentious South Kingman. R. A. Huber had lunched before taking off from Prescott and then made the uneventful 150-mile drive in two hours. It was only three-thirty when she rolled into town, an hour early for her appointment. She found lodging in uptown, not far from the Santoro residence, and checked in. The weather had turned unusually warm that day in October, even by Arizona standards, and she gratefully grabbed the bottle of water in the small fridge, compliments of the hotel. She quickly tended to the few articles of clothing that needed to be put on hangers and then went out to the balcony of her room, made herself comfortable in one of the chairs and sipped the cool, refreshing water.

Half a mile away, Inger Santoro was in a foul mood. She was pacing down the hallway of her Spanish style home as far as the den and back to the front entrance area. As she walked back and forth like a caged animal, she muttered to herself, first he tells me I can't drive to Laughlin today because we're expecting some private eye that Bruno sent our way, and then he has the nerve to take off and go fishing! He'd better show up soon, or I'm out of here. I'm not about to talk to the woman by myself.

She stood still for a second, looking at her watch for the umpteenth time in the last ten minutes, then stamped her foot in frustration and continued her pacing. In her mid-thirties, long-legged, blonde and blue-eyed, Inger was an attractive woman when she was not sulking. At the moment though, her features contorted with anger, she was not pleasant to look at. Headed toward the den once more, she heard the front door bang shut.

Turning around, she changed direction and came to a halt in front of her spouse, saying, "You sure took your sweet time to get home!"

Rocky Santoro was about to embrace his wife, but pulled back when he saw the rage in her eyes.

"What's eating you?" he asked.

"Do you know what time it is? That woman is going to be here any minute and you reek from fish."

He grinned and said, "I'm well worth the stink; you should see the beautiful trout I have in the cooler! And don't worry; I've got plenty of time to shower before the appointment with Mrs. Huber."

Inger shook her head and remarked sarcastically, "Catching a few fish is all it takes to make you happy. I envy you!"

"I'm still hoping that you'll adjust to the simple life here."

"Fat chance!"

# Chapter 12

R.A. Huber had chosen to sit on an upright upholstered chair after being ushered into the den and had declined refreshments. She now studied Rocky and Inger Santoro while they settled themselves on the couch. They made a handsome couple, she decided. His olive complexion, dark hair and eyes stood out in contrast to her fair Nordic features. Too bad that the lady seemed to wear a permanent frown on her face, Huber thought.

To put her at ease she remarked, "I like your home and your taste in furnishings."

"The house is okay, but I wish it was standing somewhere else."

"You don't like living in Kingman?"

"I hate it!"

Rocky intervened, "It's really not so bad. It's quiet and peaceful. My wife just has to get used to the different lifestyle." Looking at his spouse and patting her knee, he said, "It'll take a little time, but once you've made some new friends, it'll all work out. You'll see, Honey!"

Huber asked, "I take it you moved from the Los Angeles area. How long have you been here?"

"Six months," he replied.

"Six months too many," his wife murmured under her breath.

Huber thought, so much for trying to put her at ease! Then she said, "Now let's get to the reason I came to see you today. How well do you know Elena Campione?"

Rocky replied, "Not well. Bruno brought her along a few times, but not lately. I guess she was bored here."

"What do you think of her?"

He seemed to plan his answer carefully before he said, "She's a nice kid with great looks, but insecure."

She turned to Inger and said, "I bet you were thrilled to have someone to do chick-stuff with."

"Actually, we didn't hit if off," she replied.

Then Huber addressed Rocky again and inquired, "How did Mr. Campione find and hire you to run his newly acquired club?"

"Bruno knew that he could trust my judgment after putting me in charge of The Gem some years back when he went to Italy for his father's milestone birthday celebration and was absent for over two months."

"That was a long birthday party!"

"He was supposed to only be gone for three weeks but got sick and had to stay longer."

"Nothing serious, I hope?"

Rocky chuckled and said, "Bruno is pretty macho, so he was embarrassed when he called me and said he contracted measles or chickenpox or something from his niece. Apparently, her parents don't believe in vaccinating."

Inger stated, "It was mumps."

"Whatever." Rocky continued, "He was actually in real bad shape for a while and too weak to work after getting home. So the three weeks turned into more than two months. I didn't mind as I was in between jobs at the time."

"How were you hired for that temporary job?" Huber asked.

"I don't know what you mean?"

"Did Mr. Campione put an ad in the paper?"

"Oh, I get you! We are family; he's my cousin."

"I see." And after a slight pause she inquired, "Were you also in between jobs when your cousin was looking for someone to run his Arizona club?"

He nodded and said, "I couldn't find work and Bruno helped me out by hiring me and even set me up in this house. He won't regret it. I'll make good and show a profit with the club in no time." And disregarding the warning glance from his wife, he went on, "It's a matter of public record and you can easily look this up, so I might as well tell you; I've done time."

"I see," Huber said again.

"I have a temper and got into a fistfight, but I won't go into all that. I was only in prison for a short time for assault and battery and, believe me, I've learned my lesson the hard way."

Huber suddenly wished that she hadn't gulped all that water before getting there. She couldn't ignore the urge any longer and said, "May I use your bathroom, please?"

Inger said, "Of course! Down the hall to your left, right next to the entrance."

As soon as the lady detective was out of earshot she hissed, "Are you crazy? Why the hell did you tell her all that?"

"Bruno said to fully cooperate."

"Cooperating is one thing, telling her your life story is another! You needed to be up front with the police; no choice there since they already had you on record. This private sleuth is different and you know it!"

"You heard her questions. She smelled a rat. Besides, I couldn't think of a proper excuse why I had been jobless and - -"

Inger put a finger over her mouth, "Shush, she's coming back!"

Huber sat down and come straight to the point, saying, "I understand that on Sunday, October 12, the day that Elena disappeared, Mr. Campione stayed here with you. Did you all relax at home that day?"

Rocky replied, "No, like I told the authorities, we went our separate ways and cannot vouch for each other. Even though they assured us that Elena was only missing and as far as they knew no crime had been committed, it was obvious that they were checking our alibis.

"I'll repeat our statements to the police for you: Inger went to Laughlin for the weekend. She left Friday afternoon and came home Sunday evening. The hotel records show her two-night stay. Bruno left early on Sunday morning for two antiques and collectibles auctions, one in Flagstaff, the other in Prescott, and was back in the evening. He lucked out and bought three prints and a bronze, all to add décor to the club. The prints are already hanging and the bronze was delivered yesterday. As a matter of fact, a bunch of guys will help me put it in place today before the club opens. As for me, I went fishing on that Sunday and was also home for dinner like the others."

"Where do you go fishing, Mr. Santoro?"

His eyes lit up as he answered, "There are plenty of great fishing places on the Colorado River. Today, I took my boat to Topock Gorge where the fishing is excellent. On the Sunday that Elena went missing, I fished on Lake Havasu. I even stopped at a bar for a beer on my way home, if that counts as an alibi."

"What kind of fish do you catch?"

"Mostly bass, trout or catfish."

Huber turned to the lady of the house and remarked, "My husband and I also venture to Laughlin now and then.  We find strolling from casino to casino along the river walk most enjoyable.  What kind of gambling do you prefer?"

"I like blackjack and also play the machines."

"Shooting craps is my game."

Rocky checked the time and said, "I need to get going. The guys are probably waiting for me at the club already to help with the heavy bronze.  I'm sure Inger can answer any other questions you may have."

As he got up to leave Huber asked, "What's the place called and where is it located?  I'd like to have a look at it later, if I may."

"We simply call it *The Club*.  As for location, drive all the way through town and take Beale Street to the right of Route 66,  and keep going until you get to South Kingman. At the very end of town you'll see the red sign, 'The Club', to your right.  You can't miss it.  I'll be keeping an eye out for you!"

Then he said, "Nice to meet you," kissed his wife good-bye, and walked out the door.

# Chapter 13

Left by themselves, the two women seemed tongue-tied for a minute or two. Huber mulled over the pieces of information she had gathered from her interview with the couple and was contemplating on how best to proceed. Inger thought, what else is there for her to ask? Seems to me that Rocky told it all.

"What is your profession, Mrs. Santoro?"

"I was a party planner, but my services are not in demand here in the boonies."

"What kind of parties?"

"Oh, anything; birthdays, bar mitzvahs or bat mitzvahs, *quinceaneras*, graduations, weddings, anniversaries - - you name it. I can come up with an appropriate theme for any occasion and plan a really exciting party."

"You miss your work a lot, don't you?"

Inger nodded and said, "I got paid for having fun!"

Then Huber probed, "I gathered from your earlier remark that you don't get along with Elena. Why is that?"

"She's a flirt and trouble maker."

"Really?"

Inger hesitated for a second. Then she thought, Rocky spilled his guts, so why shouldn't I vent my feelings? She said, "I was glad that Bruno didn't take her along on his last few visits. She bugs the heck out of me. It is obvious that her husband adores her, but that's apparently not enough for Elena. She demands attention from every male she comes in contact with."

Huber started to get the picture and remarked, "How annoying for you."

"No kidding! It didn't take her long to figure out Rocky's weakness for blondes."

Huber studied the woman she faced and then visualized the photo of Elena she carried in her purse. Although Inger was a decade or so older, the two women were essentially of the same type.

"You suspect an affair?"

"Possibly, but I have no proof. The thought is disgusting; dammit, we're family!"

The private investigator noticed the younger woman's eyes welling up with tears of anger and frustration and changed the subject, saying, "Your first name and looks indicate Scandinavian descent, but you have no accent. You must be second generation, right?"

"Yes, my parents emigrated from Norway. I detect a slight accent in your speech, though. Are you German, Mrs. Huber?"

"I'm originally from Switzerland, but have been in the US for such a long time that I consider myself a full-fledged American."

Then she asked, "What do you make of Elena's disappearance? Is your gut feeling that she wanted to vanish without a trace or do you believe someone abducted her?"

"I don't care one way or another and hope she never comes back."

"No one will ever accuse you of dishonesty!" Huber commented, and got up to leave.

Inger walked her to the front door and said, "I'm curious about something."

"Yes?"

"Why do you go by R. A. Huber? I mean, what does R. A. stand for?"

"You've finally hit on something that will surely cheer you up! My name is Regula Agatha."

Inger laughed and said, "Stick to initials!"

# Chapter 14

Later that night Huber called her husband's cell phone.

"Peter! It's me."

"Hi Regula, where are you?"

"I just got back to my hotel room in Kingman. And how far up the coast did you get?"

"I'm still in Carmel. The signing here was over at two in the afternoon, so I could easily have driven farther, but you know how I love this town, so I'm spending the night." He added, "You surely are calling late!"

"Am I keeping you up? I figured you'd watch the eleven o'clock news."

"That wasn't the point of my question."

They both said in unison, "Let me tell you about my day - -" and then burst out laughing.

"You go first," Peter said.

So she filled him in on her visit to the Wilsons and also the interview with Rocky and Inger Santoro.

He heard her out and then remarked, "That Wilson guy sounds like a cold customer and a bad father. He doesn't even worry about his daughter's disappearance. All he seems to care about is his scientific projects."

"Actually, I found Marcia Wilson to be the cold fish, unless I'm misjudging her and there is passion underneath that cool exterior. I think that Ted Wilson is deeply hurt that his mother bequeathed her fortune to Elena and bypassed him. I suspect that fact is the main cause for the estrangement between father and daughter. All the other reasons he mentioned may be true, but I think they're secondary."

Then Peter asked, "Do you believe Rocky's wife - - what's her name?"

"Inger."

"Do you believe Inger is on target about her suspicion of an affair between her husband and Elena?"

"I have no idea. I wish that I could form a clearer picture of what kind of person Elena really is, but I'm fumbling in the dark."

"What do you mean?"

"Like 'Will the real Elena Campione please stand up!'"

"I still don't get you!"

"Everyone I've talked to seems to have a different image of the young woman."

"So she's wearing many hats?"

"Maybe. Or perhaps people just see her differently."

"Give me some examples."

"Okay. Andi described her as having a sweet disposition. Her father stated that Elena had a habit of running away from things rather than facing the music. He also mentioned that when in high school, she had changed boyfriends like shirts. Her younger brother calls her an airhead. Rocky tagged her as a nice kid who is great looking but insecure, whereas Inger portrayed her as man-crazy and a trouble maker. Andi called me just as I was about to dial your number, and I got the rundown of her interview with Bruno. According to him, his wife is emotionally dependent and helpless. He wants to protect and take care of her."

Peter said, "You wonder if they are talking about the same person."

"Exactly!"

"Andi seems to be keeping late hours too."

"Bruno had phoned giving her the name and number of Elena's estate lawyer, and she wanted to pass it on to me before I'm headed for Phoenix."

"The fiery tomboy from New Orleans is damn good at the job, isn't she?"

"That's a fact! I've come to depend on her and am most fortunate to have her. I'm not so sure that she would appreciate being labeled a tomboy, though. Andi has come a long way since she blew into my office at 18 on a day in January nearly three years ago. In case you haven't noticed, she is becoming a more stunning woman with every passing day!"

"Oh, I've noticed all right!"

"Now Peter, tell me about your day."

"There isn't all that much to tell. The weather has been unusually warm, so being near the ocean is great. Both yesterday and today's signings were a success; quite a nice turnout of people. Oh, there is something that you'll get a kick out of. Remember the very first book I wrote?"

"How could I ever forget *The Four Seasons With Regula*?"

"Well, a man came all the way from San Jose to hear me talk and purchased my latest book. He lingered after the signing, telling me that he was bummed that you were not with me on the tour. Apparently he was intrigued by you and had made the trip mostly in the hopes of meeting what he called 'the little lady!'"

"My absence was probably for the best. Seeing me in person may have been a big disappointment to him."

Then he asked, "Did you go to The Club tonight?"

"You bet."

"Is it anything like The Gem?"

"The floor plan is similar, but on a much smaller scale. The décor is totally different, though. You cannot compare it with the classy grandeur of The Gem. I've got to hand it to Bruno Campione; he is clever with thinking up themes and finding artworks to go with his motifs. The Club's theme is Cowboys and Wild West, and the prints he is accumulating are in black and white, but not nearly as large as the ones at The Gem. Rocky pointed out the three framed photographic prints Bruno had purchased at that auction and they are fabulous. One is of a saloon, another a bathhouse and the third a wagon train. Rocky and his men placed the impressive bronze that was delivered yesterday in the entrance hall, and it is the first thing one sees when stepping inside The Club. Remember the Remington bronze the Morgans display in their living room?"

"The cowboy riding a bucking bronco?"

"Uh-huh. This is the same Remington, only much larger. I would say about four feet high and three feet across."

"Wow! A bronze of that size definitely makes a statement. Did the club look busy?"

"It was crowded and a happening sort of place."

Peter remarked, "That's surprising. I wouldn't have thought that a nightclub in Kingman would go over that well."

"Maybe word got around that The Club was *the* place to be on a Saturday night and not only young people from Kingman, but from surrounding towns, are flocking to it." She added, "There was some line dancing going on and I joined in."

"Of course!"

"Where do you sign tomorrow?"

"Santa Cruz.  What about you, where are you headed?"

"Haven't decided yet.  Either Phoenix to see Brenda Wilson and the lawyer, or Laughlin."

"Who's in Laughlin?"

"Harrah's, the Golden Nugget, Colorado Belle, Riverside and some others."

"Oh those guys!"

# Chapter 15

Andi took her Harley-Davidson for a spin, not for an aimless ride, but with a definite destination in mind. She had phoned Elena's old boyfriend, David Driscol, on Saturday evening and asked to see him as soon as possible. He had suggested that if she was in such a hurry to talk to him, she should come to the MB2 track in Sylmar where he spends most Sundays. Then he had given her the address and directions to the place and hung up. As soon as the connection was broken, Andi had asked herself, what the heck is an MB2 track? An online search led her to the facility's website, an indoor Go Kart racing track. What'd you know, the little twerp, as Bruno called him, is into Go Kart racing, she thought.

Now she enjoyed the mild California fall weather and the carefree ride westbound on the 210 Freeway due to easy Sunday traffic. Her mind flashed back to the meeting with Bruno the day before. So it looked like Elena was somewhere in the US and penniless. As she dwelled on that, her darkest suspicion seemed to become a reality. She felt bad for Bruno; he was obviously beating himself up for having left his wife alone so often. Thinking back to the last day they had talked, Andi could not recall anything unusual in Elena's behavior. The two had walked out of their classroom together making plans for the following Thursday at Mario's, the Italian restaurant in South Pasadena. That had been on Friday before Elena drove off, and Andi was certain that her friend had not been troubled at that time. So something or someone must have triggered her to abruptly leave town by the next Tuesday.

Andi stopped her musing as the Yarnell exit came up ahead and concentrated on following directions to the race track. Having to memorize directions, rather than reading them off a piece of paper, was one of the few disadvantages a motorcyclist had to put up with. She remembered to turn right on Foothill and then another right into Balboa Boulevard. She almost passed the place up, but saw the sign with the red letters and the gray number two against the black background - - MB2 Raceway - - at the last minute. Surprisingly, the indoor Go Kart race track looked like any huge office building from the outside. Andi parked the bike and went in.

She passed the registration counter on her right and headed toward the track, where there was a race in progress. Small groupings of tables and chairs for spectators were scattered about in the large area facing the track. Andi found an empty spot and sat down to watch the race. The place was extremely clean and to her astonishment relatively quiet. The big engine noises she had expected to hear were nonexistent. She counted eight racers currently competing on the quarter mile long track of eleven turns. The numbered karts were built low to the ground with about six-inch wheels, and all of the karts were painted bright red. Andi was looking up at the lap time board, trying to figure out which one of the racers was ahead, when the flag man waived the white flag, indicating the last lap.

As the eight men filed out of the track area, removing their helmets and neck braces, one of them came straight over to Andi and said, "Hi! I'm David. You're the only redhead in the place, so you must be Andi!"

She got up and they shook hands. He was fair with a round baby face and 5'7" tall. Andi, at 5'9" and wearing her two-inch heel cowboy boots, towered over him. David Driscol was in his mid-twenties but appeared more like he was in his late teens.

Andi asked, "Did ya win?"

He looked up at the billboard and replied, "Close, I came in second."

"Second out of eight ain't bad," she replied.

"What do you think of the place?"

"I'm mighty impressed! It's amazingly clean and quiet and there's no bad smells."

David stated, "MB2 Raceway is Los Angeles County's only indoor kart racing facility. The karts are electric and therefore emission-free. They're made in Italy and are of the finest in racing quality and performance."

"Do they drive like cars?"

"Pretty much."

"You shift into gears?"

"No, they only have an accelerator and brake."

"How fast do they go?"

"50 mph."

Andi asked, "Can people bring their own karts?"

"Not at this indoor track. Racers have to use the MB2 karts provided. They need to be recharged after every race, by the way. At outdoor race tracks you can bring your own."

"I reckon that outdoor racing karts run on gasoline?"

"Correct."

"Is that the only difference?"

"It's the main difference, but there are a few others. Speed is one of them. Outdoor Go Karts are a lot faster, but they're noisy and one gets dirty racing on an outdoor track."

"You race outdoors too?"

He nodded. "I've been in races at the California Speedway in Fontana. The Los Angeles Kart Club hosts a race out there once a month and I've participated in a few."

He continued, "Go Karts have come a long way since they were first introduced. They are closely related to open wheel racing such as Indy Car and Formula One. Most professional race car drivers perfect their skills on Go Karts before advancing to auto racing."

"Are you looking in that direction?"

"I've thought about it," he replied.

The next race was under way and Andi watched, fascinated. She pointed at the karts as they sped by and exclaimed, "I'm dyin' to ride one!"

"Want to give it a try?"

"Sure do!" And she asked, "You mean, I can just rent a kart and take it on a practice spin?"

"No, you'd have to enter a race."

"How does that work?"

"It's simple; whoever is ready for the next race can enter it. Maximum ten racers can race at one time and there is no minimum. You'd have to register and sign a waiver first, though."

"What about safety equipment? Isn't there a lot of stuff I'd have to wear?"

David explained, "That is true if you were to race on an outdoor track, especially in dirt track racing. For your safety you'd want to wear a helmet, neck brace, racing suit, vest for rib protection, gloves and leather shoes that fully cover the foot and ankle. At this indoor road race track, the only mandatory equipment needed is the helmet and neck brace, which you can rent here, and close-toed shoes."

He noticed her eyeing his outfit and said, "I wear suits just because I'm comfortable racing in them, but they're not a safety requirement here.  You're perfectly fine in your jeans and leather jacket."

"Can I wear my own motorcycle helmet?"

David glanced at the helmet Andi carried under her arm and said, "You may, but yours doesn't cover the face, so you'd have to wear goggles with it."

"No problem," Andi replied, "I've got my goggles."

"They'll brief you on racing safety and regulations when you register and sign the waiver, but is there anything you want to know before you go to the counter?"

"Sure do.  How many laps do I race?"

"You'll be doing a standard fourteen-lap consumer race."

Then Andi pointed up at the board where the times for the current race were shown and said, "This is obviously a time race.  I studied the board after you finished racing and there was only one time posted for each racer.  For instance, look at the first name posted:  27.115 seconds.  That time is for one lap, correct?"

"Yes, of course."

"So why is there not a total lap time listed for all fourteen laps added up at the end of the race to determine the winner?"

"In a standard race it's a time challenge against the clock.  The object is to get the fastest *single* lap of the racing session, not a combined total."

"Gotcha!"  And she asked, "Do they also have races where the drivers try to outrace each other?"

"Sure.  A group of eight or more can purchase one of the Grand Prix races.  They have several different packages. In that case, the first kart across the finish line is the winner. They offer a slew of corporate events too." And with a grin he added, "For the price of $2,200 per hour they'll close the place to the public and you can rent the entire facility, conference rooms, pool tables, gaming systems and all."

"I'll keep that in mind!"

David said, "Go sign up, then."

So Andi went over to register, filled out the release of liability form, signed the waiver and paid for the race. After a quick briefing session, she was ready to roll.

David walked her to the start area and said, "Now remember, the racing is based on lap times. So the main thing is not to slide the kart. Make wide smooth turns, starting from far outside on entry and tight to the center of the apex of the corner, and keep the flow going wide on exit. Going too fast into turns will make you slide and slow you down."

He stopped at the gate and said to the attendant, "This is her first race," and to Andi, "Good luck!"

Surprised, Andi asked, "You're not racing?"

"I prefer sitting this one out and watching you!"

She went through the gate and grabbed a neck brace from the pile, wrapped it around her neck and secured it with the Velcro. Then she donned her helmet and goggles.

The young man in charge motioned her to an empty kart and said, "Get familiar and comfortable with the kart while you wait for the rest of the racers."

There were three karts with racers seated in them in front of her and hers was the fourth in line. She pulled herself down into the seat and felt a little strange sitting in a vehicle so close to the ground, but she was not uncomfortable. She familiarized herself with the kart, which was basic; accelerator pedal on the right, brake on the left and the steering wheel between her knees. At the briefing they had told her to be sure to obey the flags, so while waiting for the race to begin, she quickly went through the meaning of each flag in her mind. Green flag started the race; red stopped the race; yellow meant caution and slow down; blue/yellow was the command to hold line for leaders passing; a black flag indicated to a racer that he was disqualified and needed to exit the track; white signaled the last lap, and the checkered flag meant that the race was finished. Got it down pat, Andi told herself.

Five more racers had joined them, making a total of nine competitors, and the race was about to start. The flag man waved the green flag and Andi accelerated, yelling, "And away we go!"

It took her a few rounds to find the feel for it. She tended to take the turns too fast, and sure enough, each time she was sliding the kart. Braking too hard also made her kart slide out and consequently she lost time. The trick was to keep the momentum up. By about the ninth or tenth lap, she started to have better control and was enjoying herself more and more. Also, the blue/yellow flag was waved less frequently at her as fewer leaders passed by.

David was watching Andi's progress with interest. He had no trouble spotting her as her black motorcycle helmet stuck out like a sore thumb among the colorful headgear of the other racers. He had to admit, for a beginner she surely caught on fast and was holding her own.

Andi had just been telling herself, I could get hooked on this, when the flag man waved the white flag in front of her. What? The last lap already? she thought with regret.

David met her as she came out of the track and said, "Your best lap time was 32.125 seconds, pretty good for a first try!"

She blurted, "Holy Krewe, I sure had a blast!"

"Did you say crew?"

"Sure did, Krewe with a capital K."

David stared at her, dumbfounded.

"You Westerners don't know much; a Krewe is an organization that parades at Mardi Gras."

# Chapter 16

Stepping a bit away from the track, Andi chose a small table and chair farthest from the action and said, "Let's talk about Elena."

"Yeah, that was your reason for coming," David remarked, "so shoot."

They sat down and she asked, "How long did you date?"

"About a year."

"I reckon you got to know her well?"

"Better than most people, I'd say."

"I have some classes with her at PCC and consider her my friend, but she never shared much about her life in Arizona when growin' up. Did she talk to you about her kinfolk?"

"Not often, but I do know that she didn't have much of a family life. She barely saw her father as he seemed continuously holed up in his laboratory, paying little attention to her. His scientific projects evidently took priority. Still, I got the feeling that she was afraid of him. I don't think there was any love lost between Elena and her stepmother. The only person she adored was her grandma."

"Why do you think she was frightened of her daddy?"

"Part of it was that he demanded perfection, like expecting straight A's from his kids, and Elena couldn't swing it. The other thing is more complicated and has to do with money."

Andi said, "You mean it's about the inheritance she'll get from her grandma when turning 25?"

"Oh, you know about her trust. My guess is that her dad is holding a grudge."

"Let's get to Elena's current life."

David quickly asked, "Yeah, what did her husband tell you about me?"

"Not much, really. Bruno said that when he called you after Elena's disappearance to find out if you'd seen or heard from her, you told him that you hadn't talked to her in ages and had no idea where she went."

"That's all he said?"

Andi smiled and replied, "He did mention that you raised hell at The Gem one day soon after they were married."

Embarrassed, he replied, "I'm not proud of that, and having had too much to drink that evening is no excuse."

"I'm not holdin' it against you. You must've loved her very much."

He nodded and admitted, "Sometimes I think that I still do."

"How did you meet?"

"At a dance competition. She made it to third place, but I was eliminated way before."

Andi took a closer look at him. Even though he was wearing an all-covering racing suit, it was obvious that the young man had the disciplined and muscular body of a dancer.

He continued, "We started dating after that competition event, and when she got hired to dance at The Gem, I was real happy for her. Then she broke up with me a few months later, telling me that she was engaged to Campione. I was in total shock. I thought we were connected body and soul, but apparently she did not feel the same way. Sometimes I went to the club just to see her perform and then sneaked out before she even knew I was there."

"She's an above average dancer?"

"You never saw her dance or you wouldn't need to ask. Elena is a superb dancer and also an extremely good performer. Dancing is not something she enjoys doing once in a while; dancing is her life."

"I hear ya!"

"Can you imagine that husband of hers did not allow her to perform any longer after she became his wife?"

Andi said, "I kind of understand that from his point of view."

"Well, I don't. It's like taking the pacifier away from a baby. Bruno Campione is a selfish brute, if you ask me."

The young man had uttered these last words with so much force and resentment that Andi suspected his emotional wounds were far from being healed.

She gently said, "David, I don't think you told Bruno the truth when you said that you hadn't seen Elena in years."

He didn't answer right away and seemed to mull things over. Then he burst out, "Oh, what the hell! You figured it out. Yeah, I did see her a few times lately. She called me about three months ago and said that Bruno was out of town and that she was lonely. I took her dancing that evening. After that, we went to clubs together whenever he was gone." With a little smirk he added, "Of course we avoided The Gem."

"When did you see her last?"

"Let me see. It was about two and a half or three weeks before she disappeared."

"The truth now, please; you didn't see or talk to her during Bruno's *last* time away?"

He shook his head sadly and said, "She was supposed to call me so we could make plans for a date, but I never heard from her." And he had a hard time controlling his emotions when he asked, "What happened to her? Tell me you think that she's alive."

Andi replied, "I don't know, but I swear I aim to find out!"

She had already turned to leave, then swung around and asked, "By the way, what were you doing on Sunday, October 12?"

He stared and then replied, "I was here at the race track. Where else would I be on a Sunday?"

As she approached her motorcycle in the parking lot, a man was standing by her bike and seemed to scrutinize and admire it. He was so absorbed in his study that he did not notice Andi coming to a halt next to him.

When she put on her helmet and took another step forward, the person finally looked at her and said, "This Harley here is yours?"

"Yes sir, it sure is."

"I'll be damned, a chick riding a bike like that!" the man murmured under his breath. Then he said, "She's a beauty! I wouldn't be surprised if I was looking at a vintage Harley. What model is it?"

Andi replied, "A 1990 FXR Super Glide."

"Seems in top condition, too."

"Yes sir. The engine was rebuilt three years ago, but everything else on it is original."

He looked at her keenly and inquired, "You wouldn't by chance be interested in selling it?"

"Not on your life!" she replied, swung one long leg over the saddle, kicked the kickstand up, hit the starter button and put it into gear. Then she turned her head, smiled, and waved to the man as she rode off.

# Chapter 17

At that moment, four hundred miles to the east, R. A. Huber sat at the corner table of a Starbucks franchise in Phoenix, Arizona, sipping her coffee and waiting to meet Brenda Wilson. She had studied the variety of exotic brews offered and debated whether to try an Espresso Truffle or even a Peppermint Mocha, but being a creature of habit, she had ordered her standard, plain coffee.

She had a clear view of the front door and paid attention to any young woman entering who was approximately the right age. During their phone conversation Brenda had said that she would wear a red top for easy identification. So far, Huber had noticed plenty of young women wearing red going in and out of the coffee shop. The place swarmed with students from Arizona State University. She could not suppress a smile as the realization hit her that she herself would more likely be spotted and approached by Brenda, as she seemed to be the only older person present.

During the three-hour drive from Kingman she had reflected on the various bits of information she had obtained about Elena so far. It appeared that the missing young woman had a more complex personality than was originally evident, so she was curious to learn what Brenda's opinion of her sister would be.

"Mrs. Huber?"

The elder looked up at the young woman who stood next to her table and said, "Yes, that's me." And rising to her feet to greet her, she declared, "There was no need for the red blouse; you look just like your mother! I'll get you something to drink. What would you like?"

Brenda replied, "I'll fetch it myself."

Huber insisted, "My treat; that's the least I can do. After all, you're giving up your Sunday afternoon to talk with me."

"Oh okay. Then I'll have a Café Latte, please."

Returning with the beverage, Huber studied Brenda's face once more. It was true that her features strongly resembled those of Marcia Wilson, and she owned the same thick dark-brown hair, but whereas the mother came across as cold and impersonal, the daughter's brown eyes radiated warmth and kindness.

She said, "Are you enjoying college life, Ms. Wilson?"

"Yes, I am. I like the academic courses, but most of all, I love being independent and making my own choices. And please call me Brenda."

"Do you know where you're headed with your studies?"

"Yes," she replied. "I'm getting into nursing."

"That is certainly a wonderful and worthwhile profession. Your parents must be proud of you."

"Actually, they're not pleased. They both agree that if choosing a career in the medical field, I might as well become a doctor as they think I'm smart enough." With a little shrug she added, "No matter what, I'm standing firm. I'll become a nurse and that's that."

"Good for you!" Huber remarked.

"Don't get me wrong, I love my parents, but the time is over when I let them make decisions for me."

"I can see that you are a self-reliant young woman and comfortable in the role. I understand that your sister was not as confident when she was your age."

"That's true. Elena had a hard time when she was a student here at Arizona State. I don't blame her for dropping out."

"Oh?"

"She hated it here from the very beginning. Elena should have entered a dance academy and not a university. She's made for a career in dancing. Dad wouldn't hear of it and practically forced her into Arizona State. So she just miserably went through the motions until she couldn't handle the pressure any longer and took off."

Huber detected compassion in Brenda's eyes as she spoke about her sister and gently said, "You care for her, don't you?"

"Yes, we've always been close." And she shared, "Even though Elena is three years older, she usually comes to me for advice and support. She was popular and played the dating game to extremes in high school, which was her way of covering up for being insecure. I was 15 when she left for college and I prayed every day, 'Please God, help Elena cope at school.' When she had just started her sophomore year, Grammy Wilson died and that broke her heart. She was actually staying with Grammy, but after her death moved into the school dorm. No one could blame her for not wanting to continue living in the big house where everything reminded her of Grammy. A few months later she dropped out."

"She must have loved her grandmother dearly."

Brenda nodded. "Grammy and Elena were two of a kind. They shared their common interest in dancing, thought and reacted the same way, and they even looked alike. Grammy was the one who took her to ballet performances and paid for all her dance lessons over the years."

"I understand that Elena will inherit your grandmother's estate soon. How does the family feel about that?"

"Dad is mad, of course. And who wouldn't be, in his shoes? This is his mother we're talking about and she passed him up."

"What is your personal reaction?"

"I'll admit, at first I had my nose bent out of shape too, but then I thought of what a special relationship Grammy always had with Elena, and I kind of understand her reasoning."

"Have you been keeping in touch with your sister since her marriage?"

"Sure, Elena phones about every two or three weeks and comes for a visit once in a while."

Huber asked, "When was the last time you saw her?"

Brenda hesitated for just a moment before she answered, "About three months ago. She'd accompanied Bruno to Kingman. After the third day she couldn't stand being watched like a hawk by Inger anymore. Bruno dropped her off here in Phoenix and she stayed with me for the remainder of his business trip."

"I met Inger Santoro and was under the impression that she may have cause for jealousy."

Brenda shrugged and said, "I don't know about that. Lots of women are jealous where my sister is concerned, whether they have cause or not. I never met Inger, but according to Elena the woman is a real bitch."

"And your last phone conversation with your sister was?"

"About a month ago. I had planned to call her soon since I hadn't heard from her in a while when Bruno phoned, looking for her."

"Are you worried?"

"I wasn't at the time and thought that she just needed to be by herself for a while like she told him in the note." And with a sigh she added, "Now I'm starting to get concerned; she's been gone too long."

On a whim Huber asked, "Does it surprise you that she picked the balloon festival in Albuquerque for her getaway?"

"Not at all! Mom and Dad took us there almost every year for the annual October event. It was sort of a family tradition. I don't know if they still go." And with a wistful smile she added, "The balloon festival was certainly one of Elena's favorite places to go to when growing up. She once told me that surveying the balloons take shape while hot air was being blown into them, then watching them being launched and take off for the sky was like getting up and away herself."

"I see." Then Huber said, "How would you describe Elena?"

"She's fair and extremely pretty."

"I have a picture of your sister and know that she's a beauty. I wasn't referring to her looks."

"Oh, you want to know what she's like. Elena is kind and generous, but also sensitive and emotionally dependent. She'd give her last dime to a friend in need, yet must be protected and taken care of herself. She does enjoy attention from men and flirts to hide her insecurity. Her honest and true personality comes alive when she dances. She expresses her feelings better with her dancing than most people do with words." And with a smirk she finished, "Does that answer your question?"

"Yes, indeed. Thank you!" Then Huber said, "Do you mind telling me what you were doing on Sunday, October 12?"

"Let me see - - that was the Sunday two weeks ago. As I recall, I sat in my room cramming for a test that day."

Huber had no more to ask and handed over her business card with the request to call if she heard from Elena. As she walked from the Starbucks Café to her car she mused, Brenda Wilson is one mature and levelheaded young woman! And her next thought was, I wonder if I should place any importance on the slight hesitation she made before stating that she had not seen Elena in three months?

# Chapter 18

On Monday, October 27, Huber started on her journey to Albuquerque. Sunday evening she had stopped at a charming bed and breakfast on the outskirts of Phoenix. The place was so quiet and relaxing that she had overslept. There were no other guests left when she showed up for breakfast at ten o'clock. Thinking she was too late and turning to leave, the friendly proprietress had assured her that there was no problem and she would whip her something up. Minutes later, when Huber was indulging in her waffles topped with fresh strawberries, the kind lady wanted to know if her travels involved business or pleasure. Huber had replied, "My business trip seems to be turning into pleasure as we speak!"

So she had a late start when she headed North on 17 to make her connection with Interstate 40 once again. It was already two in the afternoon when she stopped at the small town of Holbrook to have a bite to eat. Driving through a stretch of flatland, she experienced gusty winds and had to reduce speed and hold on tight to the steering wheel. Some 20 miles farther and without warning, a heavy downpour began. The rain came down so heavily that visibility was extremely limited, especially with trucks passing, splashing additional water over her windshield. When the road became even more hazardous and she could not see out of her car at all, she took the next exit, tanked up with gas and waited the storm out.

Finally, she arrived in Gallup, New Mexico, at what she thought was five-thirty, but in fact it was an hour later due to the difference in time zones. She checked into a motel near the main road and then drove downtown, where she strolled around for a bit. Downtown Gallup is full of Indian artifacts, jewelry and rug stores, but they had all closed by that time. Satisfied with the cheese ravioli and spinach salad she ordered at an Italian restaurant, Huber headed back to her room and called it a night.

# Chapter 19

The deafening whistle of a train pulling into town jerked Huber out of a pleasant dream early the next morning. It had been a week since she'd seen the inside of a gym, and she was aching for physical activity. What the heck, she thought, I'm 138 miles away from Albuquerque. That's only about a two-hour drive. I can certainly allow myself some time here. Elena Campione has been missing for over two weeks now, so I doubt that it makes any difference when I arrive.

She quickly showered, pulled on her active-wear and sneakers, grabbed a banana and a glass of orange juice at the continental breakfast nook of the hotel, and went out for a morning jog. She dashed into a side alley behind the hotel building, and soon her run took her along residential areas of Gallup. The air was crisp and she was glad to have put on her windbreaker. A few minutes into her jog, the houses became sparse, and when she came to a fork in the road, she took the narrow lane on the left, which sloped slightly upward. As her breathing became more labored, her jogging changed to brisk walking. When the terrain leveled out she picked up her pace again, and scampering around a bend, she heard a voice say, "What's your hurry?"

Startled, she turned her head. An old man was sitting in front of his house, smoking a pipe. On stepping closer, she observed that the dwelling was nothing more than a shack.

He asked, "Where you headed?"

Huber stood still and replied, "No place in particular; just passing by on my way to Albuquerque."

"So what're you running around Gallup for?"

"I need my exercise."

"Bullshit! You're panting and you'll soon drop dead of a heart attack. Take it easy or you'll never get as old as me!" And patting the space next to him on the bench he ordered, "Sit down!"

Huber was going to decline his offer but decided to humor him and took the seat. After nearly three years of being a non-smoker, the tobacco smell from his pipe was still a pleasant aroma to her. This may be a test, she thought. They both turned to face one another, and for an instant Huber felt an ancient wisdom coming from the wrinkled Native American as his eyes bore into hers. She could almost hear the distant drum beat as his people sat around a fire exchanging age-old tales.

Then the spell broke and he asked, "You been to Gallup before?"

She shook her head and said, "I passed by on I-40 a few times, but this is my first stopover."

He grinned and said, "Betcha the town doesn't look like much to you, but there's plenty going on."

"Really?"

"You just missed the Festival of Cultures, and the Red Rock Balloon Rally isn't until December." He continued, "The biggest happening 'round here is the annual Inter-Tribal Indian Ceremonial. We all have a heyday then!"

"When is that?" Huber asked.

"Every August."

"Tell me about the event."

"Sure you're interested?"

"Positive!"

He took a drag from his pipe and then told her all about it. "Our people have put on the Ceremonial here as far back as 1922. For four days in a row, Indian groups and tribes from the US, Canada, and Mexico travel to Gallup to show off their talents and artwork."

Huber asked, "Which tribes?"

"Navajo, Pueblo, Apache, Comanche, Zuni, Hopi, Aztec, Laguna, and tons more."

"From what tribe are you?"

"I'm a mixture, but never mind me. Want to hear about the Ceremonial or not?"

"Yes, of course. Sorry for interrupting!"

"Gallup was an Indian place long before the white man came. Indian tribes who used to be bitter enemies in the past now come together peacefully and parade to celebrate their heredity. The big powwow in Gallup is a meeting of tribes who compete in ceremonial dances, all-Indian rodeos, and keep the Indian customs and art alive. There are arts and crafts markets and a top-class art show with judges and all. You can buy authentic Native American art and jewelry, enjoy parades, and taste our people's food."

Huber said, "You mentioned that the Inter-Tribal Indian Ceremonial is held for four days. What are some of the events?"

"There are Ceremonial parades of the tribes, the parade route going along Historic Route 66 in Downtown Gallup. This year there was a Thursday night parade and one on Saturday morning. We locals watch the evening parade, while most tourists go to see it on Saturday. The dance groups in the parade are the same ones who'll be at the Red Rock Park during the Ceremonial dances. We have rodeos in the Red Rock Park Main Arena where Indian cowboys saddle a wild pony and ride it through the arena, mount a bucking bronco, or wrestle a steer to the ground. There are also horse-pulled wagon races. Indian women from various tribes compete in wood chopping, and there is even a beauty pageant."

"Where is Red Rock Park?"

Pointing east he replied, "About eight miles that-a-way. It's North of I-40 and you take NM Highway 566."

Then he continued, "In the arts and crafts markets our people show their traditional skills in pottery and rug weaving. No two rugs are ever alike, by the way. In my younger days, I used to bring my rugs to the Ceremonial. Sheep raising and wool weaving is one of my ancestors' finest traditions. My people display jewelry made from the best turquoise, moccasins, baskets, and of course Indian dolls and sand paintings."

"The sand paintings have religious meaning, correct?"

"You got that right, woman. Every one of them is a solemn prayer."

The old man went on, "Later, on a high hill overlooking the ceremonial grounds, the tribes come together to hold their night dancing. They start with a prayer chant, and then the dancing begins. Mind you, these are not social dances. They are prayers and offerings to the gods, begging for strength and good health. There is a courtship dance too. Oh, and I almost forgot. You'd enjoy the Zuni Olla Maidens."

"Who are they?"

"They're a group of Indian women whose songs and dances have been passed down through many generations. They do the Rain Dance Song and the Pottery Dance. Rain is important to the Zuni people because it keeps crops and animals alive. The Zuni Olla Maidens carry on the tradition of asking for rain with their songs. The Pottery Dance shows their skill and graceful movement as they dance in rhythm to the beat of the drum while balancing large pottery jars on their heads. This dance honors the Zuni women's inborn strength and agility when carrying water from wells to their homes."

Huber remarked, "I'd surely love to see them perform."

He took another drag from his pipe and chuckled, "The hoop dance is highly entertaining."

"What kind of prayer does it represent?"

"None. The hoop dance is not religious; it just shows off the know-how of the dancer."

Huber asked, "I'd assume that there are war dances too?"

"Of course! The war dance is a strutting show of pride and courage before going to battle."

And finishing his representation he ended with, "Where else can you have all that at the same place in four days' time, I ask you?"

"Nowhere, I'd say!"

He coaxed, "Come back next August and I'll show you a good time!"

Getting to her feet, she replied, "I'll think about it!"

While continuing her jog, Huber realized that they had not exchanged names, which made the conversation with the elderly stranger even more endearing.

# Chapter 20

R. A. Huber had no trouble finding the Albuquerque hotel where Elena had stayed the last few days before she disappeared. The private investigator planned to spend the night but asked to see the manager before checking in. There was nothing remarkable about the man: His name was Ralph and he was in his late thirties.

Huber introduced herself and, pulling Elena's photo from her wallet, inquired, "Do you remember her?"

"Of course I do!"

"Would you answer a few questions concerning her?"

"Sure," he replied. "Let's go to my office for privacy." And he led her to a small room adjacent to the registration area.

Once seated, Huber said, "Elena Campione stayed at your hotel for a few days during the Balloon Festival, correct?"

"True, if you're talking about the woman in the picture. She registered as Susan Mason, though. I later found out from the police that it was not her real name."

"I see. So tell me all you know and observed about her."

He stated, "I normally don't give out information about our guests, but since the woman in question is missing, these are special circumstances and I'll make an exception."

"I appreciate that."

"I remember that she checked in on Thursday of the festival week and paid cash for five nights in advance. She took the shuttle bus to the Balloon Fiesta Park every morning for the next three days. The last time was Sunday, October 12, which was the final day of the festival."

"How do you know that she took the bus those three days?"

"I helped her make reservations, and I saw her leave for the bus parking lot each day."

"I understand that her room was undisturbed and her bed not slept in Sunday night and also Monday night. Why did you wait until Tuesday afternoon before you called the authorities?"

"Hey, it's a free country, lady! There is no law that prevents a young woman from staying away and spending the night elsewhere. Her room was paid for, including the night from Monday to Tuesday."

"Yes, that makes sense. Still, by Tuesday you must have been worried or you wouldn't have sounded the alarm."

Ralph nodded and said, "That's right, I did think it was odd that she stayed away past her checkout time on Tuesday, as she had inquired about a daytrip to Santa Fe. Besides, I wanted our staff to be able to clear out her room and allot her parking spot to other guests."

"Did she leave all her luggage behind?"

"It sure looked that way. There was a suitcase and her makeup bag."

"Explain the Santa Fe thing to me, please."

"There is nothing to explain," he answered. "She said that she was thinking about taking a daytrip to Santa Fe after the balloon festival was over and wanted to know what there was to do there. I gave her some tips and handed her brochures about the sites of the town."

Huber said, "I'm sure you'd usually refuse to discuss any of your guests, but we've already agreed that this is a special case. So in your opinion, was the young woman here to enjoy a vacation by herself, or was it more likely that she was in Albuquerque to meet someone?"

He took his time before he replied, "I really can't say."

"Meaning that you don't know, or that you don't want to tell me?"

He smiled and said, "I'm starting to see why you are a private detective!" He continued, "Actually, the young lady gave off conflicting vibes. She was married, and that huge diamond wedding ring wasn't my only clue. Her entire demeanor was that of a married woman, if you know what I mean. Yet she was also a bit of a flirt."

"You're extremely observant!"

He shrugged and replied, "That comes with the job."

"Did Elena, or rather Susan, as she was known to you, appear in good spirits during her stay?"

"She seemed happy enough. We chatted one day when she came back from a balloon launch, and her face glowed with excitement as she described the *Special Shape Rodeo* ascension to me."

Huber looked him in the eye and said, "Would I be correct in guessing that your interest in her went a tad beyond the call of duty?"

Offended, he shot back, "I happen to enjoy talking to a good-looking woman once in a while. There's nothing wrong with that."

"Oh, certainly not!" And on a sudden hunch she asked, "You had never met before?"

"Funny you should ask. She looked familiar, but I couldn't place her at first. Then I remembered that she resembled a kid that came here with her family years ago."

"You've got a good memory, Ralph. You must see hundreds of new faces every year!"

"That's true. The only reason she stuck out was because she was the only blonde in the family, and a beauty, I might add. The other kids and the mother were dark haired. I don't recall what the father looked like. Anyhow, it doesn't matter since I asked Susan if she had stayed with us before and she said that she had not. So I was obviously mistaken."

The private eye said, "I have no more questions. Thank you for your time. And now I had better go to the reception desk and check in."

# Chapter 21

On Wednesday, October 29, Andi parked her Harley on the Campione residence driveway behind a gray Toyota belonging to the housekeeper. Elena had never invited her to their home in South Pasadena, so this was Andi's first glimpse of it. While walking to the front door of the imposing two-story mansion, she thought, this here is housing *two* people? They must be planning a big family.

The doorbell was answered by a Latina in her forties. The petite woman scrutinized Andi from the floor up, starting with the cowboy boots, jeans, leather jacket and the helmet carried under one arm. When she looked up into the redhead's face, the stare from her dark eyes was hostile.

Andi said, "You must be Mrs. Molina. I'm Andi. How ya doin'?"

Celia Molina's expression did not soften any as she stated, "You're early. Come in." And she ushered her past the entrance area and down a hallway.

Pointing to an open door, she said, "Wait in there," and then vanished through another door.

Amused, Andi thought, so much for giving me a tour of the house! She stepped inside the room as ordered and glanced at her watch. Sure enough, she was a few minutes early for her appointment with the cleaning lady. Then she looked around the place - - what exactly was it - - a study, a parlor, or maybe a waiting room? Whatever this spot in the house was called, the three easy chairs grouped around a small round table in the center of the room looked comfortable. There was a floor-to-ceiling bookcase along one wall and a desk against another. The only thing on the desk was a laptop computer and a phone. The vertical blinds of both large windows were drawn open so that the room was filled with natural lighting. Andi heard the sound of a vacuum cleaner coming from somewhere in the house and figured she might be in for a long wait.

She was browsing the titles of some of the books on the shelves when the phone rang. After four rings, the answering machine kicked in and a woman's voice said, "Hi Elena! It's Christine. You didn't keep your appointment for the second time in a row. What is going on? Please call. In case you've lost the number, it's 795-1255." And with a final click the machine went dead.

The hum of the vacuum had stopped and Andi frantically pulled open desk drawers in search of paper and pen. There were CD disks and computer software, PC camera equipment, et cetera, but not a single scrap of paper or writing utensil. Naturally, she didn't carry a purse on the motorcycle. She also had not thought it necessary to pack her touring bag for this interview. Maybe I'll have time to store the number into my cell phone memory, she thought, and reached into her pocket. Too late! She already heard footsteps in the hallway and they were rapidly coming closer. As a last resort, she silently repeated 795-1255, storing the number in her brain instead, while quickly jumping onto an easy chair.

Celia Molina took a seat facing Andi and said, "I hate to be interrupted in my work. That's why I asked you to come after four in the afternoon when I'm done and ready to leave."

Andi checked the time. According to her wristwatch it was exactly four o'clock now, so she said, "This won't take long, just a few questions."

"The police already did their questioning, keeping me from doing my job. I had nothing to tell them and the same goes for you. The only reason I even opened the door and let you in is because Mr. Campione told me to. After all, he is my boss and this is his house."

"I hear ya, ma 'am! How long have you worked for Bruno and Elena Campione?"

"I did the cleaning for Mr. Campione long before he got married. Let me think. It'll be five years next January."

Perplexed, Andi asked, "He lived in this big old house alone?"

"Of course he didn't. He owned a condominium when he was single."

Then Andi said, "You clean the Campione residence every Wednesday, right?"

"All day, from eight to four. It's a big place."

"Did the Missus tell you that she was leavin' town beforehand?"

"No, she didn't."

"I reckon you have a key to the place?"

"Of course."

"You must've seen the note she left."

"Sure, I saw it. It was sitting on the kitchen counter when I came to clean on that Wednesday."

"What did you make of the note?"

"Nothing. I didn't read it."

"Come now, Mrs. Molina, you must've been curious enough to find out what the note said!"

She shrugged and replied, "Sometimes Mrs. Campione leaves a note for me when she wants special jobs done, like cleaning out the fridge or sponging off the upholstery. When I saw that the note was for her husband, I didn't read it as it was none of my business."

Andi thought, holy Krewe, this woman is impossible! Aloud she inquired, "Do you have other employers, besides the Campiones?"

"I have four more households to clean every week," she replied.

Andi snickered and remarked, "Betcha that keychain is pullin' you down some!"

The housekeeper was not amused. If anything, her expression became even more forbidding.

After a pause Andi tried another approach and said, "Do you enjoy working for Bruno and Elena Campione?"

"The pay is good and the house is manageable."

"What I mean is, do you like'em?"

Mrs. Molina rolled her eyes in annoyance and then said, "Yes, I like them just fine."

"You figure that they have a good marriage?"

She gave Andi another grim look and declared, "That's none of my business."

"Reckon not," Andi said and could not think of any more questions to ask the housekeeper. So she thanked her and got up to leave.

As soon as she was out the door and walking to her bike parked in the driveway, she murmured the number again, then leaned against the Harley and dialed it.

"*Timeless Dos!* How can I help you?"

"Timeless what?"

"Dos, like in hairdos," the young woman giggled at the other end.

"Gotcha!   My name is Andi and I'd like to make an appointment with Christine, please."

"For what day?"

"As soon as possible; my hair's a mess!"

"Let me see - - you said Christine, right?"

"Sure did."

"She's booked until the end of next week.  Would someone else do?"

"Afraid not.  Christine was especially recommended by Elena Campione."

"Really?  Hold on a sec."

Andi looked up at the house and thought, this is taking longer than I figured.  Mrs. Molina is gonna show me off the property any moment now!

Finally, there was a click in the cell phone she was holding to her ear, and then a voice announced, "Hello, I'm Christine.  You said Elena is a friend of yours?"

"You betcha!"

"You're in luck, I just had a cancellation.  Can you make it tomorrow at three o'clock?"

"Sure can.  Thank you kindly!  What's your address again?"

Andi listened carefully and then stored that information in her memory as well.

# Chapter 22

When Huber called Andi that evening, she learned all about her go-kart racing experience at the MB2 track. Andi seemed to have totally taken to the sport and described her entire race in detail. Huber smiled into the phone as the young woman elaborated on technique of how best to take curves to achieve maximum track time.

She said, "Glad to hear that you enjoyed yourself. Now tell me about David Driscol."

"Sorry, boss! I got carried away! Of course you want to get the skinny on him. David looks like a kid, but I reckon he's in his twenties. He's a dancer but there ain't nothin' sissy about him. That's how they met, by the way."

"I've lost you, Andi. What are you talking about?"

"Elena and David met at a dance competition."

"Oh, I get you now."

"He admires her dancing, and I'm sure he's still in love with her. He practically said so."

She continued, "I didn't learn a whole lot from him, but he admitted that he started seeing Elena again three months ago and after that took her to clubs whenever Bruno was out of town."

"When did he say was the last time he saw her?"

"Two or three weeks before she disappeared."

"Think he was telling the truth?"

Andi replied, "Guess so, unless he's not only a dancer but also a mighty good actor."

"Do you have anything else to report?"

"Afraid I messed up the interview with Mrs. Molina, the housekeeper."

"Was there a language problem?"

"Hell no, her English is better than mine. She was what you'd call a hostile witness."

Huber laughed.

"She didn't tell me a thing and minds her own business, that's for sure. I don't think she took me seriously. I got the feeling that I was just a wild bike-riding kid to her. Reckon you could've done better, Mrs. Huber." And she added, "She even denied reading the note."

"You mean the note wasn't there on Wednesday when she cleaned the house?"

"It was there all right. She saw it but claimed that she didn't read it."

"Now that is hard to believe!"

Then Huber recounted her conversation with Elena's sister and the questioning of the hotel manager in Albuquerque.

Andi listened carefully and then asked, "You think Brenda Wilson is as understanding about Elena's inheritance as she said? I mean, this is her grandma too and she's not getting any money."

"She seemed sincere, but we really don't know, do we?"

Then Andi said, "A couple of things you learned from the manager are interesting. Using a phony name to register in the hotel proves that she didn't want anyone to know where she was at."

"I agree."

"And that daytrip to Santa Fe she had in mind after the balloon festival was over and her luggage left in the room clearly shows that somebody either lured her away or kidnapped her." And her boss picked up on the sadness in Andi's voice as she went on, "I'm sure Elena is dead."

"I fear that you are right, but since her body hasn't turned up, we can still hope."

Andi had been fingering her Swiss Army knife inside her right jeans pocket. It was not a real thick one like the kind people took camping, but a Victorinox Explorer, which was the perfect size for her to carry comfortably in her jeans, yet had a slew of features. It came with two cutting blades, a corkscrew, a can-and-bottle opener, scissors, tweezers, a toothpick and more.

She now pulled it out and, admiring it, said, "Did I thank you enough for the great pocket knife you gave me for my birthday?"

"More than enough; you first hugged me when I gave it to you, and then you sent me a thank-you note!"

"Well, I just love it and use it every day."

"Glad to hear it," her boss replied. Then she said, "I'm on my way back and should arrive home by Friday. What is your next move?"

"Well, ma'am, reckon I'll ditch my last period at PCC tomorrow as it's high time I get beautified!"

# Chapter 23

The second phone call Huber made that Wednesday evening was to her husband.

"Hi Peter, it's me!"

"Hello, Hon! Where are you?"

"I'm spending the night in Flagstaff, and you ought to be in San Francisco by now, right?"

"Indeed I am, and what a glorious town it is! I'm enjoying every single minute in this city."

"How's the weather?"

"During the day it's sunny but chilly, typical of San Francisco."

"Well, it's down right cold here. Albuquerque wasn't exactly fit for sunbathing, and I've been freezing ever since I got to Flagstaff. I walked about three blocks to a restaurant for dinner and was cold to the bone even while wearing my heavy parka."

"What did you expect? It's the end of October and Flagstaff is at an altitude of 7,000 feet!" And he added, "So you're already on your way home, then. Did your visit to Albuquerque bring you any closer to tracing Elena?"

"She definitely seems to have vanished into thin air from the Balloon Fiesta Park on Sunday, October 12, but I already knew that beforehand. By the way, I spent the night at the same hotel where Elena stayed, and they even gave me her room, which had a fantastic view to the

Sandia mountains. I must admit that I was a bit on edge sleeping in the same bed as the missing woman. Early this morning, I went to the virtually empty launch field and tried to picture what it had been like for Elena to watch hundreds of balloons go up. As I was staring into the sky, someone walked by behind me and I literally jumped."

"Do you feel that your trip was a waste of time?"

"No, I wouldn't say that. It was useful in getting me ideas about the case, and I've learned more about what kind of person Elena is. On Sunday, I stopped in Phoenix to talk with her sister, and what I learned from that level-headed young woman helps me paint an even better picture."

"Such as?"

"Elena appears to have had a special bond with her grandmother and fell apart when the old lady passed away. According to Brenda Wilson, their father forced her sister to attend Arizona State University, rather than pursue her dream of becoming a professional dancer. The image that I've gathered of the missing woman is that of a kind, sweet, coquette, yet insecure young adult, who felt she was born to dance."

Peter asked, "What about those ideas of yours you were talking about?"

"They need to be sorted out. I'll have plenty of time to think on my drive home."

"Did you see Elena's estate lawyer?"

"His name is Kirk Bergstein, and I had planned to pay him a visit while in Phoenix. He was cordial enough on the phone but refused to see me. Mr. Bergstein stated that he will not talk to me or anyone else about Elena or her grandmother's will, as he does not discuss his clients without their specific permission."

"I'd say that is proper conduct on his part."

"Of course it is, but I'm frustrated on my part! Now tell me about you!"

"I didn't have a signing today, so I strolled around. I wished that I could've shared the perfect day in this great city with you, Regula. I'm staying at a hotel near Fisherman's Wharf but as usual ventured way out of the area. Remember the four-story book store on Market Street I was so impressed with last time we visited San Francisco?"

"Vaguely," Regula replied.

"Well, it is no longer there. I'd been looking forward to leafing through it, so I was really upset."

"I can well imagine."

He continued, "I explored a good part of the city on foot and towards late afternoon into early evening walked along the waterfront on Embarcadero, from Pier 1, all the way to Pier 39, ending up at Fisherman's Wharf again. I went over to look at the sea lions sitting on their wooden floats as always, some lazily sunning themselves, but a good many of them making a racket with their loud barking calls. I ended the day with dinner at Pier Market."

"Is that the seafood restaurant where we had the wonderful salmon last time we visited San Francisco?"

"The same! I was given a small window table and watched the sun set beyond the Golden Gate Bridge."

"Sounds like you had a wonderful day! So what's next on your agenda?"

"I have two more book signings in San Francisco, one tomorrow and the other on Friday. Then on Saturday, I'll head down the coast again. My last appointment will be in Santa Barbara on Tuesday evening, but I won't spend the night; I'll be driving straight home afterwards."

"Where I'll be waiting with bated breath!" his spouse teased.

She heard him chuckle and they said their good-byes.

# Chapter 24

Timeless Dos was a trendy hair salon located in South Pasadena. When Andi arrived for her appointment, the spike-haired, black-lipped receptionist told her to have a seat and that someone would be right with her. True to her word, within seconds, a young woman ushered Andi to an area where she joined other customers lined up in "shampooing chairs" with their heads bent back into basins, getting their hair washed. Andi had hers scrubbed and the scalp massaged. Then someone wrapped her hair in a towel, creating a turban. Next, she was guided to a work station where a young woman with short, straight black hair and inquisitive gray eyes was waiting for her.

"Hi Andi! I'm Christine. Sit down, please." And undoing the towel she continued, "Let's see what we've got here. - - Wow! Even wet, I can tell that you have great hair!"

"Thank you!"

"Normally, I try to talk customers into a change of color, but your shade of auburn is too awesome to mess with. Would you like to have it straightened, though? Perfectly straight hair is so in."

"I'll pass on that. Just cut some."

"Do you know what style you want or shall I show you pictures you can browse through?"

Andi thought, this is more complicated than I imagined. Aloud she said, "I don't want a different style. Just cut about two inches off."

"I see. A little trim and shaping is all you want?"

"Yes, ma'am."

Christine giggled and said, "No one's ever called me that before. I just love your Southern charm!"

Then she concentrated on cutting and shaping for a while, and Andi wondered on how best to start the questioning.

She could have spared herself the bother as the hairdresser suddenly remarked, "So you're a good friend of Elena Campione?"

"Sure am."

"How long ago did she recommend me to you?"

And while Andi was considering how she should answer, Christine continued, "The reason I'm asking is because I don't know what to make of Elena right now. She missed her appointment for a haircut about two and a half weeks ago and then called the next day apologizing for not keeping it and rescheduled. Then she didn't show up on the new date either. I can understand forgetting an appointment once, but surely not twice in a row. Besides, by now she must need a cut desperately. I'm positive that she's getting her hair done somewhere else."

Andi started to open her mouth, and again Christine went on, "I must have offended her in some way, but have no clue of what that could possibly be."

At last, Andi was able to get a word in. "Elena is not mad at you; she's gone missing." And she explained the situation and her part in it.

Christine looked at the redhead with something close to awe and exclaimed, "You're really a private investigator? How cool!"

"Only a part-time assistant. Now let me ask you a couple of questions. For how long has Elena been your client?"

"I've been doing her hair for about three years - - no, actually, it's closer to four."

"So you've known her before she was married."

"That's right. She was Elena Wilson in those days and worked as a waitress. At the time I was wondering how she could afford all the designer clothes she was wearing and she always managed to look immaculate from head to toe. She must've gotten manicures and pedicures regularly, and we're not exactly cheap here at Timeless Dos."

"Reckon not!" Andi put in.

Christine stopped cutting hair for a second and leaned towards Andi conspiratorially, saying, "Then one evening, I saw her perform at a real sleazy club in Hollywood and realized that she had a night job on the side."

"You mean she was a stripper?"

"Well, maybe not a stripper; I think it's called an exotic dancer. She put on a great show. Still I wondered, what's a classy gal like her doing entertaining in a place like that? Anyhow, next time she came to get her hair done I mentioned that I'd seen her performance, and she denied working there and said that I must have been mistaken. I'm positive that it was her, though."

Then Andi asked, "Did Elena ever talk about her kinfolk?"

"She never mentioned her parents, and somehow I got the feeling that there may be trouble there. She did chat about her grandmother who'd passed away, and I could tell that she really missed her. Then later, after she was married, she often talked about what a great guy her husband was."

"When did you see her last?"

"Let me think. That was in the beginning of September when she needed a touch-up color job and a trim. No, wait. I saw her after that, but not here. I ran into her at Macy's."

"When?"

Christine interrupted her work once more, trying to recall exactly when it had been. She finally said, "I remember now, it was a few days before the first appointment she missed, and I thought she acted a little weird."

"What do you mean?"

"As I said, I bumped into her at Macy's, in the baby department, of all places. I was there to buy a shower present for a friend when I saw Elena standing there, totally absorbed with looking at baby outfits. I asked her if she was shopping for a gift and she replied, 'No, just browsing.' I selected a present, paid for it and then passed by where Elena was still lingering at the same spot. I waved to her as I left, but she didn't acknowledge me."

"Holy Krewe! Reckon she's pregnant?"

"Either that, or wishes to be."

Then their conversation came to a halt as it was impossible to talk over the racket of the dryer. When Andi's hair was dry and coiffed, Christine handed her a mirror so she could see her head from all sides.

"Looks great!"

Christine fiddled with a lock that had already sprung out of place and said, "Glad you like it."

Then she glanced at Andi's hands and remarked, "Your nails could use some attention. We don't do manicure/ pedicures, but I can recommend a real good place." And peering at Andi's brows, she added, "They do waxing too."

Andi thought back to the one and only eyebrow waxing she had suffered through at Optimum House over two years ago and answered, "Thanks, but I'll give those parts some attention myself."

After paying, she came back to Christine's work station to hand her a tip, and the hairdresser said, "Good luck with finding Elena, and please let me know when you do."

As Andi stepped out of Timeless Dos, her hair felt a little lighter and her wallet was practically weightless!

# Chapter 25

R. A. Huber had spent Thursday night in Laughlin and on Friday afternoon, October 31, was traveling homebound on Interstate 40. She had allowed herself a bit of gambling fun, as she never shied away from combining work with pleasure. She smiled to herself as she thought of the creative Halloween costumes some of the dealers and croupiers had worn. She had shopped for candy ahead of time and hoped that she would make the drive home by the time the first trick-or-treaters would knock at her door. Shortly before reaching Barstow, her cell phone rang and a breathless and distressed Andi gave her the following update:

"Bruno Campione called. Elena's body washed up at Lake Havasu. The police informed him that the case is now a homicide and no longer a missing person."

"That's terrible news! I'm sorry, Andi. When was she found?"

"A few days ago, but I don't know the details." She sighed and added, "I suspected that she was murdered all along, but I hoped to be wrong."

"I know, and I feel for you. How is her husband doing?"

"He sounded awful. I didn't see him; he just phoned to let me know before he left for Havasu, as he needs to go identify her. I think that's just a formality because they already checked DNA and know who she is. I offered to go with him, but he wants to do the horrible task alone."

Something in the young woman's voice caught Huber's attention and she said, "Careful, Andi! Don't get emotionally involved."

There was hurt in her tone as she shot back, "I'm already emotionally involved. She was my friend, remember!"

"I think you know what I meant."

Andi ignored the warning and burst out, "We have to catch her killer, Mrs. Huber!"

"I'm on my way home. When back in town, I'll stop at the office and call you from there. Then we'll put our heads together and figure it out."

"Yes, ma'am."

As soon as they hung up, Huber thought, I wish it was as easy as I made it sound. The truth is, we are a long way from solving the murder of Elena Campione.

# Chapter 26

The meeting between the two women did not take place until Saturday. A big rig had overturned Friday evening on the 210 West and Huber was stuck in traffic. When she finally drove out of the mess, she just wanted to get home and unpack.

After reaching the office on Saturday, Andi found her boss bent over three open maps of New Mexico, Arizona and California, while using a calculator and busily making notations on a yellow legal pad. She glanced over her shoulder and read:

      Prescott to Albuquerque - 417 miles
      (approx. 6 hours)
      Phoenix to Albuquerque – 420 miles
      (approx. 6 hours)
      Kingman to Albuquerque – 470 miles
      (approx. 6 ½ hours)
      Los Angeles to Albuquerque – 788 miles
      (approx. 11 ½ hours)
Andi read on:
      Prescott to Kingman – 2 ½ hours
      Kingman to Phoenix – 3 hours
      Prescott to Lake Havasu – 3 ½ hours
      Kingman to Lake Havasu – 1 hour
      Los Angeles to Lake Havasu –

The list broke off at that point while Huber was obviously calculating the miles and hours for that last entry.

She penciled it in, looked up at Andi and said, "Sit down and let's talk."

Andi, absorbed with the list, stated, "I see. You're trying to figure how long it would've taken each suspect to drive to New Mexico, murder her and throw the body into Lake Havasu. I reckon that with "Los Angeles to Albuquerque" you had David Driscol in mind. It would've taken him two days and everyone else could've done the dirty job in one."

"Something like that, but it's not that simple. I'm going on the assumption that Elena was murdered in Albuquerque and the killer then drove to Lake Havasu to get rid of the body. It may not have happened that way at all; she could have gone along willingly and alive. In that case, the homicide could have taken place a day later or even longer. The medical examiner can determine approximately when she was killed and how, but until someone is able and willing to share that information with us, I'll assume that she was murdered on the spot on Sunday, October 12, the day she disappeared."

She added, "Aside from a serial killer, or some other nut who randomly picks his victim, we have to presume that we know the culprit."

Andi nodded, then asked, "So what next? Do we check alibis and motives?"

Huber smiled and said, "No one appears to have an airtight alibi. As a matter of fact, alibis seem to be nonexistent."

"What do you mean?"

"Let me take you on a journey of suspects. On that Sunday, Ted Wilson was sitting in his lab doing research while his wife was running errands. I didn't ask their son what he was up to on that day, but I'm sure he would have told me that he was also somewhere in Prescott. According to Rocky Santoro, he was fishing all day on Lake Havasu, his wife was hoping for a jackpot in Laughlin, and Cousin Bruno Campione was busy amassing items for his new club at antique auctions in Flagstaff and Prescott. Brenda Wilson stayed put in Phoenix the entire day, studying for an exam. Any one of them could have driven to Albuquerque in the wee hours of that Sunday morning, abducted and murdered Elena, and then made the journey to the lake."

Andi thought about this for a moment and then remarked, "Didn't you tell me that Inger Santoro had hotel records to prove she was staying in Laughlin from Friday to Sunday?"

"True, but she could have checked out really early, like two in the morning. Sounds far-fetched, I know."

"You also said that Bruno bought stuff from auctions in Flagstaff and Prescott. You even saw the pictures and the bronze, right?"

"Correct."

"So he couldn't have gone to those auctions and on the same day to Albuquerque, killing Elena, driving all the way to Lake Havasu to dump her, and be back by dinner time, now could he?"

"Sounds fantastic, I agree." Huber continued, "And you said that David Driscol claimed to have spent the day at the Go Kart race track. We didn't question Phil Drummer, the manager of The Gem, or the housekeeper, Celia Molina, about their whereabouts on that crucial Sunday. They seem unlikely killers in this case, but we cannot afford to overlook anyone."

She paused to think and then said, "So that covers all the suspects, and as far as I'm concerned, none seem to have a firm alibi."

"Guess we have to tackle motive, then."

"Okay, let's start with Bruno Campione."

Andi said, "Husbands are usually the prime suspects, but we sure can't find a motive in Bruno's case. He is well off and doesn't need her money."

"I can come up with several. There is the money angle, regardless of his own wealth, even though we do not know yet who'll inherit Elena's fortune. The motive could also be jealousy; remember, Elena was somewhat of a flirt. Or, he was a controlling and tyrannical husband and she defied him, so he followed her to Albuquerque where he killed her in a rage. Granted, this last suggestion is highly improbable."

She continued, "With Ted Wilson, as well as Marcia Wilson, the motive would be to get at the grandmother's money, of course. In Ted's case, it may also be revenge and hatred, not just greed. Money may also play a role in the cases of Elena's brother and sister, although to a lesser degree. Or there may have been strong sibling rivalry which we're unaware of. It is entirely possible that Rocky Santoro had an affair with Elena and silenced her. I can well imagine that he would want to keep such a transgression a secret from Bruno and especially his wife."

Andi nodded and said, "Inger doesn't sound like the forgiving kind."

"Then there is Inger herself. Her motive would certainly be jealousy. That leaves David Driscol - -"

Andi finished the sentence for her "- - whose reason for bumping her off would also be jealousy."

"Not necessarily. I'd say he would have been motivated by love."

"You're jivin'!"

"Not at all. Love is an extremely strong emotion and can lead to murder if mishandled."

Andi replied, "I never thought about it that way, but I guess that's true."

"As far as Phil Drummer and Mrs. Molina are concerned, I see no obvious cause for either wanting to harm Elena, but that doesn't mean that it's nonexistent."

And after a pause she said, "There is always a chance that a victim knows too much and therefore is eliminated, but I don't think we have to concern ourselves with that possibility in Elena's case."

Suddenly teary-eyed, Andi burst out, "No matter what, she didn't deserve to die!"

Then she pulled herself together and asked, "How did the murderer even know that she was at the Balloon Festival in Albuquerque in the first place? As far as we know, she didn't tell a soul where she was heading. You reckon he or she followed her there?"

"I've been wondering about that too. If she was followed, the killer would have had to start trailing her from the house in Pasadena all the way to New Mexico, which is unlikely. I think that she either confided her destination to someone or planned to have a rendezvous at her final stop in Albuquerque."

They sat in silence for a while, each mulling over their discussion. Then Andi exclaimed, "Rocky was fishing in Lake Havasu!"

"That sticks out like a sore thumb, I agree. Yet it could be a coincidence. Admitting to me that he was fishing there on that day tends to put the odds of being innocent in his favor. On the other hand, mentioning the fact may have been a clever move on his part."

"What if he just made up the fishing story in case someone saw him at the lake?"

"That is conceivable, of course."

Huber stared at the Arizona map still spread out on her desk and remarked, "Her body could have been flung into the Colorado River farther upstream, somewhere near Bullhead City or Laughlin, where the current may have carried it down to Lake Havasu. I doubt that the murderer would have bothered to go farther north than that."

Then she folded the maps neatly and commented, "This is all speculation; we really don't know a thing!"

# Chapter 27

None the wiser, the private investigator drove to her office in Pasadena on Monday afternoon, as her morning had been spent doing a couple of loads of laundry and going to the gym. As always after playing racquet ball, she felt refreshed in body and soul. During the hour on the court, she was able to empty her mind of all thought and solely concentrate on the game. Nothing existed for her except, ball, racquet, walls and opponent.

She heard the phone ring inside her office before she even reached the door and fumbled for the key in her purse. She had counted five rings when she finally hurried to her desk and picked up the receiver.

"R. A. Huber, may I help you?"

"Mrs. Huber, this is Brenda Wilson."

"Hi Brenda! You must have heard the news."

"Yes, I know about Elena."

"I am terribly sorry."

"Thank you."

"I hope you are not alone?"

"I'm at my folks' house. They wanted to tell me in person and not over the phone."

"Good."

"I wasn't honest with you the other day when I told you that I hadn't seen Elena recently. She came to see me on her way to Albuquerque and even spent the night at my apartment. My sister confided in me, and I promised not to tell a soul. Now that she is gone, I no longer think it matters if I break that promise."

Huber could tell that the young woman on the line was trying hard not to cry and said, "You're doing the right thing. Anything that you can tell me might help catch the culprit."

"I understand, and I do need to talk to you, but not here and not over the phone. I'm planning to drive back to Phoenix this evening."

"Do you want me to come see you there tomorrow, then?"

"I know it's out of your way, but - -

"No problem; I can make the drive in less than six hours."

"I don't have any afternoon classes, so anytime after twelve o'clock is fine."

They settled on one-thirty. Brenda gave her address and directions to her apartment, and they ended the call.

Huber stared at the phone for a while, lost in thought. Brenda must consider the information she had about Elena important, or she would not expect her to make the long trip to Phoenix. There was no use to speculate on what that could be, so she gave up guessing. Then she thought, I might as well make extra use of my journey to Phoenix. So she got out Elena Campione's file and then reached for the phone once more.

# Chapter 28

While packing her overnight bag again that evening Huber called Peter to fill him in on the latest happenings. Upon hearing the news about Elena, he pointed out that this had to be expected, and when his wife shared that she and Andi were frustrated at not making much progress in their investigation, he was confident that they'd get a break soon. He felt let down, though, as his spouse explained that she would take off again the next day for Arizona and would not be home to greet him.

He said, "Now Regula, are you sure this is worth your while? You just came back from there, for crying out loud!"

"I'm disappointed too and would have loved to stay home with you tomorrow night, or better yet, drive to Phoenix later and have you join me. But what Brenda has to tell me might be important, and my gut feeling tells me that there is no time to lose at this point."

"Have it your way, then, but in that case I'll stay in Santa Barbara after the signing. No need to rush home to an empty house."

She continued, "I also talked to Kirk Bergstein today and he is willing to see me now."

"Who is Kirk Bergstein?"

"The Wilson family estate lawyer."

"Of course. I remember you mentioned that he's also in Phoenix and would not give you the time of day before."

"Well, now that Elena is dead, he reconsidered and I have an appointment to talk with him tomorrow. I'll meet with Brenda first and then see the lawyer in the late afternoon."

"Sort of kill two birds with one stone."

"You got it."

Peter teased, "So where or what are you chasing after Phoenix and when can I expect you back as my lawfully wedded wife?"

"If you play your cards right, that should happen right after dinner on Wednesday!"

Then his tone became serious as he said, "And Regula, be sure to pack your pistol."

After hanging up, Peter could not shake the worried feeling that had crept into his mind. He had heard the edge of excitement in his wife's voice and was sure that her current case was coming to a close soon. He had sensed her adrenaline speeding up right through the line. Oh, Regula! Be careful and stay safe, he silently pleaded.

# Chapter 29

Andi's day had not gone well so far. She had hardly been able to study for her chemistry test over the weekend, as her mind was on the murder case. When she left the classroom on that Monday after second period, she was certain she had flunked the test. She also expected a call from Bruno. He had said that he would give her the details on his meeting with the authorities at Lake Havasu City as soon as he came back from there.

She was pretty antsy by six in the evening when he finally called, so she quickly hopped on her bike, making the ride to his house in South Pasadena in record time of six minutes.

When he opened the door, she was shocked at the sight of him. He looked like he hadn't slept in days, with deep circles under his eyes, his hair standing out in all directions, and wearing rumpled clothing. Andi hung her leather jacket on a hook in the entryway and then followed him down the hall to the drawing room. Even his stride seemed dejected. He motioned her to a chair and then flopped into his.

Andi could imagine that Elena's body was in bad shape after it had been dragged and banged up in the river. She said, "Must've been hard, huh?"

"It was awful," he replied. "The first thing I did after identifying her was puke." And he fought for control over his voice as he continued, "She was pregnant."

"Oh Bruno, I'm so sorry!"

Neither felt compelled to speak for a while. Andi needed to digest this piece of news and Bruno seemed to be far away with his thoughts.

At last, Andi broke the silence and asked, "Did they tell you how and when approximately she was killed?"

"As to how, they told me that she was strangled and dead way before hitting the water. She was found Sunday the 26th, and the coroner did his initial examination on Monday the 27th. He put her death at approximately two weeks prior to that Monday."

Andi did the math and said, "So as we thought, she was killed around the 12th. Who found her, by the way?"

"A couple of teens going for a swim."

Bruno had been staring straight ahead during their entire talk and now he looked Andi in the eye and admitted, "I have the feeling that I'm a prime suspect. At least the police interrogated me some more and I had to go over the same ground with them again as to where I'd gone and what I'd done on that blasted Sunday. When I was leaving the building, I caught a glimpse of a couple rushing by me on their way in. I've never met them, but I have seen a picture of Elena's parents and I'm sure it was them." He added, "I guessed that they were about to be grilled too."

"Who's handling the case anyhow? Is it the police in Havasu, Albuquerque or our guys here?"

"I'm not sure whose jurisdiction it is, but they seem to collaborate and share information. I initially called the Pasadena Police Department when I reported her missing, but I don't think they're in charge any longer."

Then Andi told him about the phone call Huber had received from Brenda and that her boss was planning to drive back to Arizona early the next day to talk to Elena's sister and the estate lawyer.   She was not sure if Bruno had even listened to her when she ended with, "So I hope that whatever it was that Elena confided to Brenda will bring us closer to catching the murderer."

All of a sudden, he lost control and burst out, "Why didn't she tell me that she was pregnant?   I don't understand!  This must be a nightmare and I'll wake up at any moment."   Incapable of further speech, he ran his fingers through his unkempt hair in a helpless gesture.

On impulse, Andi reached over and touched his hand. Then, without either being fully conscious of the fact, they were in each other's arms.   At first it amounted to nothing more than a prolonged hug, but as they found one another's mouths, the kiss became passionate and urgent. Andi started panting as Bruno slowly unbuttoned her blouse.

Then he abruptly stopped himself and pushed her away, thinking, what on earth is the matter with me? Elena is dead and here I am already attracted to someone else.

Andi, for her part, had come to her senses as well and was now having similar thoughts, giving herself a mental slap in the face.

She felt utterly embarrassed as she said, "This was all my fault, I'm sorry."

"It takes two," Bruno replied.  And after a pause he added, "Let's pretend the last few minutes didn't happen and go back to where we were before."

Andi nodded, and then asked, "You've eaten supper yet?"

"No, I'm not hungry"

"Well, I'm starving and you need to eat too." And getting to her feet she said, "So where's the kitchen?"

While showing her the way he protested, "There's no food in the fridge. I haven't had time to shop."

"Betcha I'll find something!"

True to her word, she dug up a couple of eggs, some flour, a little milk and cheddar cheese. Then she applied herself to making two omelets.

Later, when straddling her Harley parked in the driveway she thought, what almost happened in there? And a picture of her late Daddy entered her mind. He was shaking a finger at her saying, "Shame on you, Antoinette LeJeune!"

# Chapter 30

Kirk Bergstein sat in his law office in Phoenix on that same Monday afternoon, doing some soul searching. After agreeing to see R. A. Huber, he had started to have qualms. Should I at least call Ted Wilson and inform him of the appointment, he reflected. After all, he was the trustee until the daughter's next birthday, and now her death shed a different light on the matter.

His original client, of course, had been old Mrs. Wilson, and since she had passed away, his confidentiality and loyalty had belonged foremost to Elena. When the young woman was only missing, his path had been clear and there had been absolutely no reason to talk with the private investigator. Now that they were dealing with a homicide, he felt that he had the young woman's best interest at heart by agreeing to talk with the sleuth. In hindsight, giving the matter some more consideration, he was wondering if he had made the right decision.

His thoughts turned to the eccentric old lady who had come to his office years ago to discuss the terms of her will and testament. The then-existing will, which was drawn when her husband had still been among the living, was simple enough. Old Wilson had left all of his considerable estate to his wife and in the event of her passing, to their only son, Ted Wilson. That day, the old lady came to change the terms of her will. It was strange how she had insisted on leaving most of her fortune to her granddaughter who was in her teens at the time and only a small portion of it to her son. When prompted for her reason, Mrs. Wilson had replied that her son was an old stick-in-the-mud and that he would only throw the money into his scientific research. Furthermore, she had made it clear that she disliked her son's second wife. "That woman is ruthless where money is concerned, like all lawyers," she had stated and then winking at him had added, "No offense, sir."

At least he had eventually talked her into setting up a trust until the grandchild was 25. At first, she had rejected the suggestion, saying, "Young man, I plan to be around for many more years, so Elena will have to wait for her inheritance until she'll be in her thirties or even forties." That she had addressed him as "young man" had brought a smile to his face, as he had been 54 at the time. Three years later, Mrs. Wilson had died of a massive stroke at the age of 69.

Kirk Bergstein scratched his head and sighed. He hated to find himself in this dilemma of being torn between loyalties.

His mind finally made up, he summoned his secretary and said, "Get me Ted Wilson in Prescott on the line, please."

# Chapter 31

At seven the next day, Huber left her house in Merida and headed once again toward Phoenix. Driving long distances came as second nature to her, and even though her mind was elsewhere, she had no trouble concentrating on the road.

She thought about the phone conversation she had had with Andi on the night before. Sunday, October 12 seemed to have been the fatal date for Elena. Huber had assumed this all along, but now the coroner's findings confirmed that theory. She wondered if the fact that the young woman had been pregnant had any bearing on the case. After dwelling on that point some more, she came to the conclusion that it did indeed make a difference. It was kind of Andi to have called David Driscol to let him know that Elena's body had turned up. The young man's reaction when hearing the sad news had been a bit strange. As per Andi, he had said, "Maybe I won't have any more sleepless nights now and can go on with my life."

Huber had stopped for a big breakfast to avoid taking the time for a prolonged lunch, and later exited at a rest area to briefly stretch her legs and use the restroom. She felt like she had traveled on Interstate 10 for an eternity. A while ago she had driven past the town of Blythe, and after that, the US-60 junction leading to Prescott. I am well into the state of Arizona now and about two hours away from Phoenix, she thought, reaching into her bag of trail mix propped up on the passenger seat. She popped a handful into her mouth and then washed it down with a few sips of water.

Aware that she tended to drive above the speed limit, Huber always made it her habit to be on the lookout for possible Highway Patrol vehicles, behind, ahead, and beside her. Glancing into her rearview mirror now, she realized that a large silver SUV had been driving behind her for a long time. She asked herself, wasn't a silver car just like it also on her tail before she had stopped at the rest area? Surely I must be mistaken! The driver probably just likes my speed and has his cruise-control set the same.

Checking out the vehicle in her mirror again, she got a glimpse of a driver in a cowboy hat. Is this person following me or am I getting paranoid? Only one way to find out, she thought, and tapped her brake and then slowed to 60 miles an hour. The SUV behind her did likewise. Then she stepped on the gas and soon was doing close to 80, keeping an eye on the rear mirror. The distance between the two cars had not changed a bit. She repeated the maneuver a couple of times while other cars were passing them. There was no doubt any longer that she was being tailed.

Was there more than one person in the SUV? Could teenagers possibly be getting their kicks by playing games trying to frighten her? At least that is what she told herself. She stayed at a reasonable speed of 70 for a mile or so, with the pursuing car following closely. When she saw an exit coming up ahead, she waited until the last minute and then swerved out onto the exit ramp, feeling confident she would be able to lose the pursuing car. To her horror, she heard deafening screeching of brakes behind her as the SUV skidded over the raised, unpaved ramp-border on two wheels and then raced after her.

The exit she had chosen took both cars out into the countryside, with no other motorists in sight, and the only sign of civilization was a small town over a mile away. That was stupid of me, she thought. I should have stayed on the freeway.

There was no question any longer of someone playing games; this was serious, and she realized with growing terror that Elena's killer was chasing her.

# Chapter 32

She told herself, okay old girl; stay cool and don't panic. You've been in tight spots before, so find your way out of this one.

She had slowed down to about 40 miles per hour as the road they were on, although paved, was full of pot-holes. She was contemplating which to drag out of her purse first, the phone or her pistol, but the cat-and-mouse play began before she got the chance to grab either. The big silver vehicle first gave her a shove with its bumper from behind, and no sooner had she recovered than it drove up beside her, trying to force her off the road. She held on tight to the steering wheel and sped up a bit to get out of the way and then kept to the center of the road, as there was no oncoming traffic and the middle of the road gave her better control. Then the car drove up to her right and attempted to ram her from her passenger side. This type of assault continued, and each time Huber avoided being driven off the road by a narrow margin, her pursuer attacked her anew from a different angle.

She knew that her Buick did not stand a chance to survive the impacts of the big driving machine in the long run, and her only hope was that they would encounter another car, or that she could hold on until reaching the town she had spotted in the distance. Soon, her reactions to the continuous onslaughts became pure reflex and instinct. Then she saw the road ahead going downhill and at the same time curving, and she knew that she had run out of luck. She purposely slowed down and braced herself for the impact.

The driver of the silver SUV waited for the exact moment when Huber was steering the Buick into the turn, then accelerated and drove into her car from the rear, pushing it over the edge of the road and down a ravine where it overturned twice and finally came to a halt 40 yards into the slope. As the airbag was activated and just before she lost consciousness, R. A. Huber's last thought was, Thank you, God, for a good life.

The driver in the cowboy hat stopped and looked in all directions to make sure no other car was approaching before stepping out and walking over to the edge of the road. The Buick below looked totaled and there seemed no movement coming from inside. She's either dead or dying, the culprit thought, and should she survive, she'll at least be out of commission for some time. In any event, I'll get a head start. And now I'd better get the hell out of here.

The villain walked back to the SUV and checked it out. There was a good-sized dent on the front bumper and the area above, but not worth worrying about. When starting the engine, he saw an approaching car in the distance and quickly made a U-turn, headed back towards Interstate 10, and then continued in the direction of Phoenix.

# Chapter 33

"It surely is loud - - sounds like sirens - - what are sirens doing in heaven?  Must be hell, then."

"Did she say something?"  asked the paramedic, holding an IV bag up above the patient's head.

His colleague, who was busy monitoring Huber's vital signs, replied, "I doubt it; she's barely breathing."

"Guess she's lucky some guy found her right after the accident.  That road doesn't exactly lead to Grand Central Station."

"What made her drive off the road out here in the boonies, with no apparent hazard in sight, anyhow?"

"Beats me."

"Maybe someone was trying to kill her and forced her off."

"You've got some imagination!  It's all those murder mysteries you're constantly reading."

The driver turned off the siren at that moment, using only the flashing lights, as the ambulance merged onto Interstate 10, heading for the destination of Quartzsite, Arizona, where the nearest hospital was located.

In Phoenix, Brenda Wilson was getting impatient. She had expected Mrs. Huber around one-thirty and the woman was now over an hour late.  She could at least call if she was delayed, Brenda thought.

So when her doorbell sounded moments later, she rushed to answer it, then stood in the doorframe and exclaimed, "Oh, it's you!"

"Well, aren't you going to ask me in?"

# Chapter 34

Andi was coming back from taking her aunt's golden retriever for a jog on Wednesday evening when the phone rang. Slightly out of breath, she picked up the receiver.

"Andi? It's Peter Huber."

"Mr. Huber! What a pleasant surprise to hear your voice. How was your book-signing trip?"

"I'm afraid I have bad news."

Andi's heart started pounding as she said, "It's not Mrs. Huber, right?"

"She's been in a car accident."

"Is she hurt bad?"

"She has head injuries with severe concussion as well as broken ribs and a broken arm."

"Oh, no! She's gonna be all right, though?"

"I don't know, Andi."

"Can she talk?"

Quietly, Peter replied, "She's in a coma."

"I'm so sorry, Mr. Huber." Then she willed herself to be calm and asked, "Do you know what happened?"

"Not really. There is an investigation in progress, but there are no witnesses to the accident. Regula apparently exited the freeway in a remote area on her way to Phoenix and drove her car off the road, down a slope, and into a ditch. I hope that she'll regain consciousness soon and can tell us why."

"Wait a minute! Mrs. Huber took off for Phoenix yesterday mornin', so when and where did she have the accident?"

"Around noon yesterday, she was approximately 40 miles past Blythe. The authorities tried to reach me, but I didn't get home from my trip until this morning when I picked up their message on my answering machine. I'm with her now."

"Where?"

"At a hospital in a town called Quartzsite. I drove the 265 miles in less than four hours."

"How are *you* holdin' up Mr. Huber?"

"Not too well, and we'd better hang up now because I need to call my son and daughter. I'll give you my cell phone number."

She wrote it down and then asked, "What can I do?"

"Pray!" he replied.

After Andi had recovered from the shock, she applied herself to some serious thinking. Why would Mrs. Huber exit off the freeway in the middle of nowhere? The whole thing made no sense. I don't even know where Blythe is, let alone Quartzsite, she mused. Reckon I'd best find out!

Turning on her laptop, she logged on to the web. Then she did a MapQuest search for driving directions from Quartzsite to Phoenix. The distance was 130 miles and the estimated driving time two hours. Granted, Quartzsite may be 20 miles away from where the accident happened, but she was sure that her boss would not have left the freeway around noon anywhere near there, when she had an appointment to see Brenda Wilson in Phoenix at one-thirty, unless she had a damned good reason.

# Chapter 35

Peter sat at the edge of the hospital bed in room 325 looking at his spouse of over forty years. Her cheeks appeared as white as the bandages covering her scalp and forehead. The right arm was in a cast, and God only knew what else lay broken below the sheet. When the doctor had initially informed him of Regula's condition, Peter's mind had been in a haze, refusing to take it all in. Besides, the physician had used so many technical and medical terms which were impossible for a layperson to comprehend. He had mentioned the word "trauma" a lot and that she had lost a considerable amount of blood, but the rest was all a blur to Peter.

He stroked her good arm gently and pleaded, "We've gone through a lifetime together; don't leave me now, Regula. I need you more than ever!"

There was no stirring in the limp body lying next to him on the bed.

He sighed. Might as well get the calls over with. He looked at his watch. It was a little after seven, so he decided to call his son first as the time was three hours ahead in New York City. Ben's initial reaction to the news was alarm and worry, but he soon comforted his dad by saying, "Mom is a tough cookie; she'll come out of this, no doubt!" Then he asked if he should fly west, but Peter assured him that there was no point in doing so at the moment. Before they hung up, Peter promised to call back as soon as there was a change in his mother's condition.

Then he braced himself for the call to his daughter, who tended to be overly dramatic:

"Hi Deborah! It's Dad."

"What's wrong? Is Mom okay?"

He hesitated for a second, trying to find the right words.

She did not wait for his answer and continued, "You always call me Sunshine, and now it's Deborah, so I know something terrible must have happened."

"Mom was in a car accident."

"Oh my God," she shouted, "tell me she's not dead!"

"Please calm down. Your mom is alive but has sustained serious injuries."

"What kind?"

"Head wounds and broken bones."

"Are they giving her enough pain killers? Is she in good spirits?"

"She's unconscious."

"Oh my God! At what time was the accident?"

"Yesterday around noon."

"Yesterday!" she yelled hysterically into the phone, "and you're only calling me now!"

Peter had no choice but to explain that he had been on his last day of the book-signing tour when her mom had started on a journey to Phoenix, and that he had not known about the accident himself until that very morning.

Deborah said, "Why was she driving to Phoenix in the first place? No, don't tell me. I suppose she was chasing after criminals, as usual. I knew that sooner or later she'd get hurt. It's insane to do the things she does at her age!"

Her dad did not respond to that outburst.

Then she asked, "Are there more injured people, besides Mom? I mean from the other car."

"There was no other vehicle involved in the accident as far as I know."

"What? No collision?" Again, she got no reply and said, "Oh, I see, she had a blowout."

Reluctantly, Peter told her the little he knew about the circumstances of the accident.

She heard him out and then said, "Driving off the road without provocation; that doesn't sound like Mom. It's more likely that someone shot at her."

After a pause she said, "I want the truth, Dad. How bad is she?"

Peter glanced at his motionless wife on the hospital bed and whispered, "I'm hoping for the best."

"I'll have to figure out what to do with the kids, but I'll fly out of Sacramento tomorrow morning and come down. What hospital is she at?"

"Don't do that, Sunshine. First of all, your mom is in a coma and wouldn't know you. Secondly, we're not in any hospital in the L.A. area, we're in Quartzsite."

"Where the heck is that?"

"Somewhere in Arizona along Interstate 10."

She finally let go and sobbed. Then she said, "I'm sorry I yelled at you, Dad. That's my way of dealing with stress."

"I know, Sunshine."

"This must be awful for you. You're right there with Mom. How does she look?"

"Peaceful."

"Will you call me as soon as she wakes up?"

"Of course, dear."

When Peter had pushed the off button on his cell phone, he thought, please God, *let her wake up.*

# Chapter 36

The night nurse had flitted in and out many times like a guardian angel, monitoring Regula's vital signs. Peter was slumped in a chair facing the bed and had tried to stay awake but was near exhaustion, dozing on and off all through the night. When the first hint of morning light crept into the hospital room, he straightened up, opened his eyes, and instinctively focused them on the figure stretched out on the bed. Did he detect a slight tremor going through her body or was it wishful thinking on his part? He rushed to her side and squeezed her hand. Then he saw a flicker of her eyelids.

"Oh Regula, you're coming out of it! Hang in there; I'm right here!"

She didn't open her eyes, but murmured, "It's heaven after all. Peter couldn't possibly be in hell."

"What did you say, Hon?"

She did not respond.

"Talk to me!"

She lay motionless again. Frantic, he pressed the call-light button.

They were changing shifts at the nurse's station and it took Jackie, the day nurse, a minute before she could get to room 325. Peter was impatiently waiting for her as she pushed the door open.

He yelled, "Do something! She woke up and now she's gone again."

The unperturbed Jackie examined the patient for pupil reaction and then calmly replied, "Looks like she's coming out of the coma; that's a good sign. I had better call the physician, then."

"But she went right back into it," he protested.

"That's common and nothing to worry about. She'll be doing that for a while before she'll stay conscious."

Tears of relief were streaming down Peter's face as he grabbed the astonished nurse and gave her a bear hug.

# Chapter 37

Andi called later in the day and was elated to hear that her boss had shown signs of recovering.

She asked, "So was she able to tell you what happened?"

"I'm afraid she's not quite back to making any sense and is slipping in and out of consciousness. The nurse assured me that this is normal, but I'd say that we're not out of the woods yet."

"Has she talked at all?"

"A little; she's been babbling about heaven and hell."

Andi tried to cheer him up and said, "Sounds like the Missus is turnin' evangelical on you!"

"I'll take her any way I can at this point," he joked back.

Then she got serious and said, "I've given Mrs. Huber's accident a lot of thought. I think Elena's killer wanted to stop her from getting to Phoenix and forced her off the road."

"You think the information Elena's sister has is that crucial?"

"Either that, or what the estate lawyer knows."

"I forgot that Regula was going to see him too. Yes, that makes sense. You could be right."

"I also think that Mrs. Huber has a good idea who the murderer is, and her trip to Phoenix would've confirmed her suspicion."

Peter said, "Wait a sec! How could the person know that she was on her way there? Even if he or she somehow stumbled on that fact, the exact time Regula would be on that stretch of Interstate 10 could not have been foreseen by anyone, let alone that she would take that particular exit. So how could the culprit even plan an ambush?"

"I haven't figured that out yet, but I'm sure Mrs. Huber didn't exit willingly."

"I see your logic now."

Andi announced, "Anyhow, I'm taking over. I'll be riding to Arizona tomorrow."

"Don't you have any classes?"

"I'm ditching school; this is more important."

# Chapter 38

Although weak and by no means out of danger, R. A. Huber stayed awake for slightly longer periods and even opened her eyes a few times, all through the day. By afternoon, she was starting to focus on her surroundings and seemed to recognize her husband. Peter had talked to the doctor in charge once more and was told that, while still in critical condition, his wife was showing progress. When asked if it was possible to transfer her to a hospital in Southern California, the physician had advised against it as he felt the patient was not stabilized enough to be transferred yet. He recommended to wait a few days before attempting such a move and suggested that meanwhile Peter should find lodging in town.

In the evening, Peter checked into a motel only a five-minute drive away. The nurses assured him that they would call immediately if there was any change. When he was informed of Regula's accident, he had not even unpacked from his coastal trip, except for his toothbrush and electric shaver. So he had tossed the two items back into his carry-on plus a couple of fresh shirts and underwear, and hurried to Quartzsite. Now, as soon as he reached his motel room, he threw the overnight bag onto the bed and stretched out next to it, and then promptly fell asleep fully dressed.

Early Friday morning, he indulged in his first shower in 48 hours, and by seven was back in the hospital room at Regula's side.

She opened her eyes, and he said, "Good morning, Hon!"

"Hi Peter! Sorry I wasn't home to greet you."

Overwhelmed, he took her in his arms.

"Ouch! That hurts!"

"Sorry! Oh, Regula, you're finally back. It was agony to watch you unconscious and then when you came too, you didn't make any sense."

"How long was I out of it?"

"Since Tuesday, and today is Friday. Then he asked, "How do you feel?"

"Tired and sore." And touching her bandaged scalp with her good hand she asked, "Do I have a head left?"

"You have a concussion and some surface wounds."

"That figures."

"Do you remember what happened?"

"I was in a car accident, but I can't recall the details."

Peter was aware that her speech had started to slow, and he realized that all this talking must have worn her out. So he said, "Why don't you rest for a while. It will all come back to you eventually."

"Good idea," she said as her eyelids were closing.

Peter gazed at her relaxed face and thought, you'll be fine now, I just know it.

Without opening her eyes, Regula suddenly murmured, "By the way, Peter. You look dreadful! When did you eat last?"

Startled, he replied, "I don't remember."

"Get yourself some breakfast, then."

"You bet!" he replied, and whistled all the way to the hospital cafeteria.

# Chapter 39

Bret Robinson, officer of the Arizona Highway Patrol, had been waiting to talk to the accident victim for three days. He had periodically checked with the hospital staff to inquire if the patient was able to give a statement and the reply had always been in the negative. He called again late Friday morning and learned that Mrs. Huber was now capable of talking, so he hurried right over.

When he got to room 325, he almost collided with the patient's physician, who was just leaving.

The doctor said, "You may talk to her, officer, but make it brief. The lady is still extremely weak and should not be excited in any way."

"Thank you, doctor. I'll keep that in mind."

He stepped into the room and first addressed Peter, "I'm sorry to interrupt, but would you please wait outside while I take her statement."

"I'm her husband and I'd like to be present."

"Sorry, sir, but you need to leave."

Regula's voice came from the bed, "Go ahead, Peter. A walk will do you good."

So he gave her a peck on the cheek and reluctantly made his way out the door.

# Chapter 40

The officer said, "Thank you, ma'am. My name is Bret Robinson and I'm with the Arizona Highway Patrol. This won't take long. Let me start by jotting down your personal information." So he asked for name, address, telephone number and so forth and filled in the blanks on his form.

Then he said, "Do you remember how your accident came about, Mrs. Huber?"

"I didn't at first, but now I recall it all," she replied. "Someone pushed me off the road."

"How do you mean?"

"He or she came up behind me and drove into my car full speed, forcing me off the edge of the pavement."

"I need details of how that came about."

So Huber told her entire story and concluded by saying, "Once airborne, it all happened in an instant, but I do remember hitting my head while tumbling, and feeling like being in an upside-down roller coaster ride before I lost consciousness."

"Did you get a good look at the driver?"

"Not at all, the face was hidden by a cowboy hat. Besides, each time the car pulled up even with me, I put all my attention on steering clear of the attacks and keeping my eyes on the road."

"Was the driver a man or woman?"

"I couldn't tell."

"What kind of car did the person drive?"

"A silver SUV."

"I meant what make,"

"I don't know, but it was certainly big."

"Did you see the license number?"

Huber shook her head and immediately regretted doing so, as the movement caused her head to throb.

"Can you tell me anything at all about the driver or the vehicle?"

"I'm afraid not."

Bret Robinson cleared his throat and said, "There must be thousands of silver SUVs' driving on Interstate 10 every day, and drivers wearing cowboy hats are not uncommon in the state of Arizona."

"I'm aware of that, officer."

"Have you any idea why anyone would want to drive you off the road?"

"I'd say to keep me from reaching my destination, which was Phoenix."

"Ah, Mrs. Huber, at last we seem to make progress!"

"Oh?"

"We naturally looked through your purse for I.D. and possible clues at the scene of the accident."

She quickly said, "I have a permit for my pistol."

"I know; we found that too. You also carried a few of your business cards, and that is what I'm getting at."

"I see."

"Am I right in assuming that your trip to Phoenix had to do with a case you are currently investigating?"

"Correct."

"So you know, or at least suspect, who the person in the silver SUV was?"

Huber had a strong suspicion of who the culprit might be, but no real proof to back it up. Discussing her hunch with this young officer now would be premature and may even get her into trouble.

She said, "I don't know any such thing."

"At least tell me where exactly on I-10 you were when you first noticed that someone followed you."

She had to think about this and set her mind back to Tuesday before the accident. She finally said, "I know it was after I had driven past Blythe and the intersection of Highway 95 - - oh, and I even remember having gone farther than the turnoff going toward Prescott. I can't recall the highway number at the moment."

"US-60?"

"That's it."

R. A. Huber's speech had gotten lower and lower in volume, and her last answer was barely audible. Officer Robinson also realized that she could scarcely keep her eyes open any longer. He must have really tired her out, he concluded.

He said, "Thank you, Mrs. Huber. I'll let you rest now. Call us if anything else comes to mind."

"Okay," she murmured.

# Chapter 41

The day got off to a bad start for Andi. She woke up early to the steady rhythm of raindrops hitting the trashcans lined up beneath the window of her room. Shit, she thought, hope it stops before I take off.

She sat at the kitchen table, spooning down a bowl of Cheerios while listening to the relentless downpour outside. Her aunt was already on her way to work but had left her a note which read: "You'll have to forget about going to Phoenix today. You can't ride the bike in this storm or you'd be soaked in a matter of seconds. See you tonight."

Andi scribbled at the bottom of the note: "I'll wait until the rain eases off some, but then I'm riding. I'm likely to spend the night in Arizona, so don't worry if I don't come home."

Later, Andi stood at the window looking out. She was ready to leave but the storm was still raging, and judging from the black clouds overhead, there seemed no end in sight. Might as well try to reach Brenda again while killing time, she thought. Before she had a chance to get to the phone, however, it rang.

"Hi Andi! Bruno here."

"What's up?"

"You're not taking the motorcycle to Phoenix in this weather, are you?"

"Sure am! I'm waiting for it to lighten up."

"It won't! I checked the forecast and it'll rain all day, and by afternoon the storm is going to spread to Arizona. I've decided to give you a ride."

"No, I can manage."

"I'd really like to come along. You're not the only one anxious to hear what Brenda and Kirk Bergstein can tell us. I sure as hell want to know too!"

Andi suddenly realized what sitting tight, unable to help catch his wife's killer must be doing to him. She felt a rush of empathy. Still, she hesitated.

"I don't think that's a good idea."

"If you're worried about spending the night, it goes without saying that we'll book separate rooms. I'm not taking no for an answer. What's your address?"

Meekly, she gave it to him.

"I'll be there in twenty minutes."

# Chapter 42

Andi stood under the covered front porch of her aunt's house, sheltered from the rain. When Bruno pulled his two-seater Porsche onto the driveway, she made a dash for it and jumped into the passenger seat before he had a chance to peel himself out of the driver's side to offer her his umbrella.

After tossing her touring bag into the trunk, he said, "Sorry about the small car. My other one is in the shop, and I can't bring myself to drive Elena's BMW."

"You're jivin'! I never sat in something this cool in my life," she replied. "Betcha this baby easily goes up to 120 miles an hour without much shaking!"

"I don't know. I never had the urge to find out."

The rain was relentless, pounding hard against the roof of the Porsche as they traveled east on the 210 Freeway. Bigger vehicles, especially trucks, splashed the small car with pools of water as they drove through puddles alongside it.

Bruno said, "Do you know what day it is today?"

Perplexed, Andi replied, "Friday, of course."

"Yes, Friday, November 7, Elena's birthday. She would've turned 25 today."

"I'm so sorry!"

They kept silent for many miles, and then Bruno asked, "Did you let Brenda know that you're coming?"

"I called last night and again just before you picked me up, but only got her answering machine. She must be in class. I don't have her cell phone number, so I'll try again when we get closer to her area."

"What about the lawyer?"

"I did reach him. Naturally, he was shocked to hear about Mrs. Huber's accident and agreed to see me instead. I have an appointment at his office at three. What I had in mind was to get to Brenda's place around two and talk with her first, but if I can't get a hold of her before then, we'll switch it around and meet with Mr. Bergstein first."

After they had merged onto I-10 and had driven along it for a while Andi said, "Something just occurred to me. If we'd keep going on this road we'd end up in New Orleans."

"You get homesick, don't you?"

"Every now and then."

Then she remarked, "Elena came along here too on her way to Albuquerque. I wonder if she made the detour to her sister just to visit, or if she had a reason for seeing her."

"We're about to find out."

# Chapter 43

Soon after stopping for lunch near Blythe, Andi said, "I reckon we're getting close to Quartzsite. I'll quickly check on my boss," and she pulled her cell phone from the pocket of her jeans.

"Hello, Mr. Huber! It's Andi."

"Hi there, and how nice of you to call."

"I can already tell by your voice that Mrs. Huber is doing better!"

"That's a fact! She has made tremendous progress since we talked yesterday. She's been alert all morning and even gave her statement to the Highway Patrol Officer a short while ago. And Andi, you were absolutely right; someone did force her off the road. She remembers it all now. As she's doing so well, I'm hoping her doctor will agree to a California transfer by Monday."

"That's wonderful news! And guess where I'm at?"

"Somewhere between Pasadena and Phoenix, I'd presume?"

"Yeah, we're close to Quartzsite; just a few miles away!"

"I take it you had to exit to make the call. Wait a minute, did you say 'we'?"

"Yes, sir, Bruno Campione is with me. It was raining buckets at home, so he kindly offered me a ride in his Porsche."

"Lucky girl!"

Andi said, "I'd like to stop by and say hi to the boss since we're in the neighborhood. We can't stay but a few minutes because I have an appointment to keep in Phoenix."

"Actually, right now is not a good time for you to visit. Regula's session with the officer exhausted her, and she fell fast asleep as soon as he left a few minutes ago."

"That's okay. We'll stop on our way back, then. By the way, did she recognize the jerk who drove her off the road?"

"Apparently not. It's hard to identify someone whose face is obscured by a big cowboy hat."

"That figures! Nothing is ever easy. See you tomorrow, then. Meanwhile, give Mrs. Huber a big hug from me."

# Chapter 44

When his wife opened her eyes an hour later, Peter said, "You missed Andi going by here on her way to Phoenix. She and Bruno are headed that way to continue the business that you started on Tuesday."

Huber sat bolt upright and exclaimed, "Stop them immediately!"

"You think they're in danger?"

She slumped back and attempted to nod but felt excruciating pain shoot up and down her head.

Unaware of her agony and mystified by her agitation, Peter said, "Surely the villain wouldn't attempt to run them off the road too; he'd be pressing his luck!"

Huber tried to raise her voice again, but only a whisper came from her lips when she said, "Listen to me, Peter! Have the officer put out an APB."

Peter asked, "You really think that's necessary?"

Frustrated at his reaction, she tried to raise her head off the pillow but failed.

Her next words were slurred and barely audible, "Stop them - - danger - -"

With a last tremendous effort she lifted her good arm and pointed at the door. Then she closed her eyes.

Peter thought, she's been through a lot and is overly dramatic now. Regardless, he went to find Nurse Jackie and asked, "How do I get in touch with Officer Robinson?"

# Chapter 45

Andi pushed the off button on her cell phone and sighed with relief.

"How's she doing?" Bruno inquired.

"She's going to make it!" Andi replied with obvious jubilation in her voice.

"What did he say when you asked if Mrs. Huber recognized the culprit?"

"She didn't see his face."

"That's too bad!" Then he said, "I can tell that you like Mrs. Huber a lot."

"Sure do! She's the greatest, and I couldn't ask for a better boss. Looking at her, you'd never dream of the things she's good at."

"Such as?"

"We went to the shooting range a while back, and I saw first hand that she's an incredible shot, even though she hardly ever carries her piece. She's a real wizard at detecting too. I betcha she's figured out who the killer is; she just isn't telling yet."

Bruno commented, "The lady is also an excellent driver; her reflexes behind the wheel are astounding for someone her age!"

"I guess that comes from years of playing racquet ball and - - hold your horses. What do *you* know about her driving and reflexes?"

She gasped as the truth hit her and shouted, "Holy Krewe, I nearly had sex with a murderer!"

Bruno realized his blunder as soon as the words left his mouth, and there was no way to take them back now. He glanced at Andi. Disgust and hostility were written all over her face.

"You no-good son of a bitch," she hissed at him.

"You don't understand!"

"I understand, all right! You should've become an actor. I truly believed that you loved Elena and all the other crap you dished out. You sure fooled me, playing the grieving husband and all!"

"I did love her!"

"Give it up, Bruno; I'm wise to you now." And after a moment's pause she burst out, "You killed your own baby, you monster!"

"That's where you're wrong. The bastard wasn't mine!"

Andi did not respond.

Bruno felt compelled to tell his story: "In many ways Elena was like a child and needed guidance, but I didn't mind and actually enjoyed the role as her protector. From the very beginning, though, I had made it clear that I would not tolerate infidelity. So for two and a half years we had a good marriage. I was going to surprise her and take her to Italy for a birthday present. However, our lives changed the night before I left for Kingman on that Tuesday, October 7. She told me, full of excitement and bliss, that she was pregnant and couldn't understand why I wasn't overjoyed at her news."

"So you knew all along that she was pregnant! And why weren't you overjoyed when she told you?"

"Because I am sterile."

"How do you know?"

"The doctor said so. I had the mumps as an adult."

"Oh."

He continued, "Anyhow, when I questioned Elena about who the guy was that she was cheating with, she insisted that there was nobody and that the baby was mine. I demanded to know with whom she was having an affair, but she just stared at me with her seemingly innocent baby blue eyes. We went round and round until late into the night, but she stubbornly stuck to her lie. Even after I explained that I could not produce kids, she still refused to confess. It was past midnight when I finally gave up and told her that we'd discuss the matter after my return from Kingman."

"You never told her before that you couldn't father offspring?"

"No."

"I find that hard to believe."

"The subject of kids never came up. I didn't think she was interested in having any."

"What happened next?"

Bruno took up his tale again and went on, "I told the truth when I said that Elena was still asleep the next morning when I took off. My mind was on the news that she had sprung on me and I was unable to concentrate on anything else. I only realized that I had left my cell phone on the kitchen counter when I wanted to call Rocky two hours into my drive. So I turned around. When I got to the house, Elena wasn't there and I could tell that she'd left in a hurry. The door to the big hall closet stood open and I noticed that one of the suitcases and her make-up bag was gone. In the bedroom she had left some clothes in a heap on the floor. It certainly looked as if she had decided to skip town. That made me angry. Was she planning to be gone when I came back from Kingman so she wouldn't have to discuss the matter any further, I wondered.

"Then I saw that the computer was on in the study. I was positive that I'd turned it off before I'd left that morning. Elena must have used it, I thought. Was she in such a hurry to get away that she forgot to shut it down again? I was curious enough to check what was typed into the search engine last. She was checking out the balloon festival and hotels in Albuquerque, New Mexico."

Bruno was full of rage and, without being aware of it, stepped on the gas pedal hard, making the Porsche take off like a bullet.

He said, "Can you believe it? Instead of facing the music, she was taking off to frolic at some freaking balloon festival!"

"Watch your speed!" Andi warned.

He took his foot off the gas and continued, "I made the decision to kill her then, although I planned the exact details later. Elena's car was gone, so I knew she was driving to Albuquerque. When taking a plane, she always called a cab to ride to the airport. Rocky expected me that day and knew that I'd stay for about a week. I had to come up with a perfect blueprint for the murder and an airtight alibi. I figured I'd have plenty of time during my drive to Kingman to think out a good plan. For now, I shut down the computer and picked up after Elena, so it would look like she had left in an orderly fashion. When I got to the kitchen to grab my cell phone on the way out, I thought of writing the note. I carefully printed it the way Elena would, and then left it on the counter for Celia Molina to see when she'd come to clean on Wednesday."

# Chapter 46

From the instant that Bruno had revealed himself as the killer, Andi knew that she was in great danger. She now remembered the advice Mrs. Huber had given her a long time ago. Her boss had said that if she'd ever find herself alone with a criminal and there seemed no way for her to escape, to keep him talking. Villains usually enjoyed bragging about how clever they'd been in their scheming. "This will give you time to form your own plan of action," she'd said.

Andi turned to her adversary at the wheel and asked, "So how did you pull it off?"

"It was easy, once I'd formed my plan," Bruno replied, continuing with his morbid story.

"I assumed that Elena would stay in Albuquerque until the end of the balloon festival, so I picked Sunday, October 12, as the target day, having the two auctions in mind for an alibi. I left Kingman in the middle of the night and made the drive to Albuquerque in a little over six hours. Inger went away to Laughlin, so I didn't have to worry about waking anyone up when leaving the house since Rocky sleeps like a baby. I'd told him that I'd be leaving early for the antique auctions, so he didn't expect me to be there when he woke up.

"There were two Albuquerque hotels earmarked on our computer at home. I decided to check the one closer to the Balloon Fiesta Park first, and bingo, that was it! I saw Elena's BMW in the hotel lot as I drove by and parked my SUV across the street at a strip mall. I snacked on a granola bar because I had no idea when I'd find time for my next meal. It was six in the morning, but I didn't have to wait long. Soon she came out of the hotel lobby and, to my surprise, didn't go to her car but crossed the street and walked straight towards me! She didn't seem to pay attention however and went right past me, looking into the distance, apparently without noticing me or the car. So I followed on foot at a safe distance."

He continued, "She stopped at a huge parking lot a couple of blocks away, obviously joining the crowd waiting to take the bus to the Balloon Fiesta Park. To my astonishment, they were all school buses. I realized that most people already had their tickets, Elena included, and were forming a line to board the next school bus. I quickly lined up behind a couple who purchased their fare from a booth on site and paid for the bus and entry fee to the Fiesta Park. I was one of the last passengers boarding the school bus. Elena was way ahead of me, going toward the rear of the bus and never looking back. I slumped into a seat in front of a fat guy, who I was sure blocked Elena's view from me. When we got off at the Balloon Park, a woman was collecting my ticket and another handed me a program. I was happy to grab the brochure to hide my face behind it."

"Elena never saw you?"

"Nope, and I followed her to the launch field and stood close behind her the entire time as she watched the mass ascension of balloons."

Andi said, "She ended up in Lake Havasu, so you couldn't have killed her there. How did you get her to come with you?"

He laughed, and the sound was not pleasant. Then he said, "I had actually thought of doing the job right then and there in the midst of the crowd, and leaving her on the field, dead. All the spectators' eyes would be focused on the sky, and chances are that no one would have noticed. It takes a very short time to strangle someone, you know! In the end, I didn't want to take the risk. Just one single person could have looked my way at the wrong moment and I'd have been in big trouble. Besides, I wanted to give Elena one last chance to confess."

He laughed his nasty laugh again and said, "To answer your question, she came along like a lamb. Of course she was surprised to see me at first. I explained how I traced her to Albuquerque because the news about her being pregnant wouldn't leave me any peace of mind, and that we needed to talk things over. I suggested that we take my car and as I said, she came willingly. Then I drove us to a secluded spot at the outskirts of the town, stopped the car and turned off the engine. We stayed in our seats and I asked her again who her lover was. I guess she was too dumb to realize that her life depended on telling me the truth. I would have spared her, had she shown any kind of remorse."

Anger was rising up in him again as he said, "But no, she did no such thing. She looked at me with her big eyes and stubbornly insisted that the child she was carrying was ours. So I grabbed the piece of cord I had ready in my pocket, wound it around her pretty neck, and pulled it tight. She struggled some, and even scratched my hand with her fingernails, but it was over relatively fast."

Andi covered her mouth with both hands in order not to scream or vomit; she was not sure which urge was stronger.

Bruno nonchalantly continued, "The rest was a piece of cake. I carried her to the back of the SUV and rolled her up into the painter's drop cloth I had spread out earlier. Then I closed the lid and drove off. It was already early afternoon when I got to the antique auction in Flagstaff. I had told Rocky that I wanted to be at the auction first thing in the morning so I wouldn't miss the three prints I had seen in the preview. I was lucky; the prints I was interested in obtaining had not been auctioned off yet. I had to wait over an hour, though, until they came on the floor. There were other interested parties, but I outbid them all. I surveyed the worker as he carefully wrapped each artwork and then loaded all three onto a dolly and I showed the way to my SUV. Together we lifted them into the vehicle and placed them over the rolled up drop cloth."

"Holy Krewe, you put them on top of Elena!" Andi yelled, unable to contain her sense of shock.

"At four o'clock, I arrived in Prescott. The most valuable objects are usually held back until close to the end of an auction, and I knew that it would be over by five. I was hoping to be in time for the bronze depicting a cowboy riding a bucking bronco. Luckily, soon after I got there, the bidding for it started. It cost me a bundle, but I'm the proud owner of that bronze now."

He went on, "It was after seven when I got to Kingman, dead tired and hungry, but I had to go through with the rest of it before I could relax. I first dropped the prints at The Club and told Rocky I'd go out to grab a bite to eat, and then I drove away in the direction of Bullhead City. I found an isolated area a little upstream from the town and dumped my rolled up package into the Colorado River. Once back in the car, I had the bright idea to call home and left that message for Elena, telling her I'd be coming home the next day. Finally, I drove back to a restaurant in Kingman and sat down to dinner."

# Chapter 47

The storm seemed to have followed them to Arizona. Ever since they had driven past the town of Quartzsite, it had been raining on and off. They were about one hour away from Phoenix. Mesmerized by the windshield wipers' rhythmic swishing, Andi frantically tried to think of a game plan. To say that her options were limited would have been an understatement. Her touring bag, with her piece tucked inside, was in the trunk of the Porsche. Trying to call 911 would be an obvious choice, but she knew that Bruno would never give her that chance. She had to think of something before getting to Phoenix. Somehow she felt her odds were better on the freeway. In the meantime, keep the creep talking, she thought.

So she asked, "What about Mrs. Huber? How did you know she was driving on I-10 at that particular moment?"

"Simple, I followed her from home."

"What do you mean, from *home*?"

"When you came to my house on Monday after I returned from Lake Havasu, you told me that your boss had received a call from Brenda and that she was going to drive to Phoenix early the next day to talk to her and also to the estate lawyer."

"I remember, but at the time I didn't think you'd been listening to a word I said."

"On the contrary, I paid keen attention." He continued, "I'd been to the office, of course, but I didn't know your employer's home address, just that she lived somewhere in the San Fernando Valley, and I assumed that she would take off from there. She was real easy to find. There is a 'Huber, P and R,' listed in Merida, and I figured that it must be her old man and her. To be on the safe side, I got to their place at the crack of dawn and waited in my car a few houses away. I could've slept another hour and a half; she didn't drive out of her garage until seven.

"At first, I kept my distance when following her, but it was tiring to keep an eye on the Buick, making sure there was at least one car between us. After we had both stopped at a rest area, I stayed close behind her, hoping she'd eventually panic. I didn't have a definite plan; all I knew was that I couldn't let her reach Phoenix."

He laughed his dirty laugh and said, "She obliged by taking a rural exit, and the rest is history."

"So who was it you didn't want Mrs. Huber to see, Brenda Wilson or Kirk Bergstein?"

"Brenda, of course. I was worried about Brenda ever since you so cleverly deduced that Elena had made a detour to Phoenix. That could only mean one thing, namely that she had paid her sister a visit on her way to Albuquerque. Out of all the people in her family, Brenda is the only one she was close to and may have possibly confided in. Thinking about what Brenda might know caused me to have sleepless nights. You see, in order to successfully playing the innocent, I had to be sure that people thought I was unaware of the pregnancy. As the days since Elena had vanished turned into weeks and Brenda did not come forward, I started to relax, thinking that she didn't know anything after all. Imagine the shock I had when you unwittingly clued me in on Brenda's phone call and that

Huber was hustling to Phoenix to hear what she had to say!"

Andi asked, "I'm curious, why did you hire us in the first place?"

He answered, "I didn't think you women were any good, and it seemed a great idea at the time. I knew that sooner or later Elena's body would turn up and thought that hiring private investigators would give me an edge."

"What do you mean?"

"You don't get it? Guess I'll have to explain. It would turn suspicion away from me because it would look as if I were so concerned about the disappearance of my wife that I'd take the trouble to hire a private detective outfit to find her. "

Andi kept silent, and he went on, "Turns out that I underestimated you two a tad, but I'm not worried."

"Really?"

After a pause he said, "I was holding my breath a while ago when you had Huber's husband on the phone and asked him if she'd recognized the driver of the SUV."

Andi replied, "Mrs. Huber may not have identified you as the driver, but I'll bet she's figured out that you're Elena's killer."

"I doubt that, and even if she has a hunch about me, she certainly can't prove a damn thing."

"You forget that Brenda is surely going to tell her story."

There was that laugh again as he said, "Why do you think she didn't answer the phone?"

"Oh no!"

"I feel bad about it, but I had to silence her."

Andi struggled with a wave of nausea and willed it to go away, saying, "Tell me about Brenda, then."

"There isn't much to tell. After I had put Huber out of commission, I continued my drive to Phoenix. Brenda didn't seem particularly scared of me, even though I'm sure she knew what was coming. We talked for a few minutes, and as I suspected, Elena had told her sister about her pregnancy. She also said that I had accused her of infidelity and claimed the baby wasn't mine. According to Brenda, my wife was afraid of me and couldn't understand what had gotten into me. Elena didn't tell her sister where she was headed and made her promise not to let anyone know that she'd stopped by. I pressed Brenda for the name of Elena's lover, but apparently she even told her sister that there was none.

"To my astonishment, Brenda didn't put up a fight at all. I'd have thought she'd be the type to go kicking and screaming. The strangling was over and done with in a few seconds."

Andi fought back her distaste and said, "So you dumped Brenda into the Colorado River too?"

"Why should I? There was no need to remove her from the apartment. I made one minor mistake, though, but I don't think it matters."

"And what's that?"

"I meant to take away the cord, but I left it with her."

# Chapter 48

An Arizona Highway officer behind the wheel of the patrol car going east on Interstate 10 said to his partner, "Isn't there an APB out for a Porsche with California plates?"

"Yeah, that's right."

"There's a Porsche two cars ahead of us. What's the license number we're looking for again?"

His partner checked and then said, "It's a personalized number, GEM 2."

"Let me get closer - - Yep, I can clearly read it now, that's it, GEM 2."

"Okay, let's call it in."

Seconds later, the officers got the order to wait for backup before apprehending the vehicle.

Inside the Porsche Andi said, "What about me? Am I going to end up in the river?"

"You've certainly got spunk," Bruno replied. "I wish that things had turned out differently for you and me. I really like you, Andi! What I had in mind when I picked you up this morning was for us to go to Brenda's place and discover her body together. I've been searching for news, but there's no mention of her in the media, so I assume that nobody has found her yet. Too bad that I made that blunder a while back."

"You didn't answer the question."

"Well, my spunky redhead, you've obviously figured out that I can't let you live now that you know it all! So how does the following plan grab you? We split up once we get to Phoenix. Not really, but that will be my story. I'll tell the authorities that we got into town late because the storm had slowed us down and that I dropped you off at Brenda's and went to see the lawyer by myself. Then I'll say that after the consultation with Mr. Bergstein, I drove back to Brenda's apartment to get you, and that no one answered my ringing of the doorbell, so I tried the door, which was unlocked. Next I'll get dramatic and state that I entered and to my horror found both Brenda and you dead. I'll assure them that I didn't touch a thing, but immediately sounded the alarm."

He cleared his throat in an exaggerated manner and then stated, "Here is the real deal. We go to Brenda's and I'll do the necessary deed. Then I'll take your place for the visit with Mr. Bergstein. I'm sure he'll talk to me; after all, I'm an interested party too. If not, I'll tell him that you'll be coming to see him shortly. The rest is the same, of course. I'll get back to Brenda's and call the police from there, reporting the two murders."

He took his eyes off the road for an instant and studied her face. Then he said, "Don't even think of trying anything funny once we get to Phoenix. I'll guarantee the outcome would be more painful for you than if you let fate take its course."

Andi had not given him her full attention during his bragging of how he would effectively eliminate her, as her mind was racing. She was desperately trying to come up with a good excuse to get Bruno to open the trunk once they got to their destination. She needed to be able to grab her touring bag and get at the Derringer. Without her pistol, she didn't stand a chance of surviving. She came up with several ideas, only to reject them again, one by one. It had to be a good pretext, or he would see right through it, and she would only get one try at it, of that she was sure.

She thought, I'd better have a brainstorm soon. We're getting ever so close to Phoenix.

Aloud she said, "What were you going to do if it hadn't been raining this mornin'? I bet you'd have tried to sweet talk me into taking you along anyhow, or were you going to stay put and hope for the best?"

His laugh was more sincere this time and he said, "At this stage of the game I could leave nothing to chance. When you called yesterday to let me know that you were going to Phoenix to follow up on Mrs. Huber's lead, I almost asked if I may join you. Then I curbed the impulse, as I knew you'd turn me down. I needed to know what was going on with your boss, though. Remember, you told me that she was coming out of the coma but was still incoherent. I guessed that she'd soon recall what had happened, and I needed to know if she had recognized me as her attacker. I couldn't possibly go to her husband for the information, so my only way of finding out was through you."

He continued, "My plan was to call you in the morning and pretend that I had decided on the spur of the moment to come along. If you'd have refused my company, I'd have made you promise to at least call me periodically to keep me abreast of your progress."

He grinned and said, "You can imagine my relief when I woke up and heard the heavy rain this morning! I may not know much about motorcycles, but it stands to reason that riding one in a storm is not much fun."

A couple of minutes later, she fumbled through her jeans pocket.

Bruno immediately turned to look at her and said, "Careful, you'd better not be reaching for your phone. Forget about calling anyone or even text messaging!"

She pulled out a couple of loose Kleenex and replied, "Just blowing my nose."

"You're not crying, are you?"

She quickly produced a sneeze attack and sniffled, "Of course not!"

Then neither spoke for a few miles. Andi was keenly aware that her antagonist was quick minded and seemed able to stay in control in any situation. He was also a cold-blooded murderer, and she knew that unless she stayed calm, she would surely be his next victim.

All of a sudden, they were surrounded by patrol cars, lights flashing.

Bruno said, "Damn it!" And then, "Okay, I'll make a run for it; you can judge for yourself how easily my little Porsche can accelerate to 120 miles per hour!"

Before he had a chance to put his words into action, Andi's hand shot up, clutching her Swiss Army knife, blade extended, from where she had been hiding it behind the Kleenex.

She raised it to his throat and commanded, "Pull over!"

With three Highway Patrol cars on his tail, two on the left lane beside him, and a knife pointing at his jugular vein, Bruno had no choice but to follow her order.

# Chapter 49

Two days earlier, on Wednesday morning, the resident doctor at the Phoenix Community Hospital looked down at his patient and said, "You are a lucky young woman, Ms. Wilson."

"I know," Brenda replied.

The physician shook his head and stated, "I don't think you are fully aware of how close you came to dying. If your friend hadn't found you and administered CPR yesterday afternoon, you and I wouldn't be having this conversation."

"Believe me, doctor, I am immensely grateful to her."

"Your parents were notified and I understand that they are on their way to Phoenix."

"I'm sure there's no need for them to come. I'm totally fine now and I was hoping to get discharged today."

He said, "You see, I have a bit of a problem. When police are involved, there are certain procedures we have to follow through. We need to find out what really happened. A specialist will have to see you first and --"

She interrupted, "You think I tried to kill myself. You've got to be kidding!"

The police report that he had looked at a short while ago came to the physician's mind and he replied, "That seems to be the general idea, but you and I know differently, Ms. Wilson, don't we?"

Brenda said, "I certainly know differently, but I have no idea what you're implying. And speaking of the police, I need to talk to them urgently."

"You were not awake when the officers came by, but I'm sure they'll be back."

He continued, "You played an extremely dangerous game. Thank God you had the presence of removing the cord before you lost consciousness, otherwise I doubt that your friend would have been able to bring you back. I'm sure you learned a hard lesson and it will never happen again."

"What on earth are you talking about, doctor?"

He just stared at her.

"Oh my God! I know now what you're thinking. I've heard of students getting a high from choking themselves. You're dead wrong!"

"So tell me what happened."

She was mad now and shouted, "A man was strangling me, that's what! I played dead before it was over, so he let go and left. I must have passed out anyhow, because the next thing I remember is waking up here in this room."

The doctor was speechless for a second and then said, "I jumped to the wrong conclusion, please forgive me." And he asked, "Do you know the man who attacked you?"

"Naturally I do! Why else do you think I'm in such a hurry to talk to the police?"

"By all means, we need to call them back right away."

# Epilogue

At the end of February of the following year, Bruno Campione's trial came to an end. He was convicted of murder in the first degree of his wife, Elena Campione, attempted murder of Brenda Wilson, and sentenced to life in prison.

R. A. Huber's bones had healed and her health had been restored, except for an occasional headache. In order to take care of her wounds, they had partially shaved her head in the hospital, so to make it uniform, she had cut off the rest of her hair after she was released. Now that her salt-and-pepper hair had reached the length of 2 ½ inches she decided to add to the drama by teasing it straight up.

That evening, the Hubers took Andi to the Cajun restaurant *Andouille* to celebrate the outcome of the trial. They picked her up at her aunt's house, and she was wearing a dress for the occasion.

As soon as she stepped into the car the older woman said, "You look stunning!"

Andi grinned and replied, "And you are hip with your hair all spiked, Mrs. Huber!"

When seated at the New Orleans style restaurant, all three ordered jambalaya.

After tasting a few bites of the spicy stew Peter said, "So Andi, is this jambalaya as good as yours?"

"No sir, I fix a meaner one!"

"What exactly is *andouille* anyhow?"

"It's a hot sausage; you're eating some in your jambalaya right now."

The conversation came to a halt while they heartily dug in and savored their food.

Then Andi said, "I'm sure glad it's over and Bruno's being put away for good! With the fancy team of attorneys he hired to get him off the hook, I was worried for a while."

Her boss stated, "Your testimony and Brenda's is what did the trick!"

"By the way, why weren't you called to testify, and why was he not charged with your attempted murder too?"

"The prosecutor felt it was best not to put me on the stand since I couldn't honestly say that I'd recognized Bruno Campione as my assailant when he pushed me off the road."

"Something else I've been wanting to ask; how did you get the Highway Patrol to come out in full force to pull us over in the Porsche? It couldn't have been just a standard alert since they apprehended us with a total of five patrol cars!"

"Actually, I cannot take full credit for that. Brenda made her statement to the Phoenix authorities after waking up in the hospital, and consequently they were already looking for Bruno before I urged Peter to have Officer Robinson put out an all-points bulletin on him. The way I understand it, he was considered a fugitive when the police could not get a hold of him at his house, at The Gem, or in Kingman."

Peter said, "Interesting what was revealed at the trial about the police keeping a lid on Bruno's attempt to strangulate Brenda. After the young woman named him as her attacker, they made sure nothing leaked to the media while he was still at large."

Then Andi asked Huber, "When did you start suspecting Bruno as the murderer?"

"From the beginning, I felt that there was something fishy about the note that Elena supposedly had left behind. If she wanted to keep her whereabouts a secret, why bother to write a note to her husband? He would sooner or later come to the conclusion that she had left and would report her missing, regardless of any note from her. And why would she care about all that in the first place if she ran away? So I asked myself, assuming that Bruno was the villain, had he either written the note himself or did it not exist and he made it up? But what purpose could this possibly serve? It made no sense to me for a long time.

"Then later, when scrutinizing people's alibis for the day Elena had disappeared from the balloon festival, I wondered how any of the suspects could have known where to find the young woman, short of having followed her to Albuquerque. At that point I figured that the abductor, if there was such a person, must have known or suspected where Elena was headed. So that note came to mind again. Did he have an inkling before leaving for Kingman that his wife would skip town and did he turn around, maybe that same day, driving back to his house to place the note there to prove that he had not been home when she left? But again, that seemed absurd, as he could not expect anyone going to their home before his return from Kingman.

"And then I suddenly realized that he wrote that note so the housekeeper would later attest that the piece of paper was already there when she cleaned on Wednesday of that week. He took a chance, though, the cleaning lady could have sounded the alarm right away before Elena even got to her destination.   Then again, he probably knew Celia Molina well enough to assume that she would mind her own business and keep quiet."

She continued, "Telling us about an alleged phone conversation he had had with his wife on Friday, three days before she disappeared, was one of the biggest mistakes he made.  Why would Elena even have her cell phone turned on if she wanted to be left alone?  And if she had forgotten to shut if off, why answer when Bruno called?  Of course, from his point of view, he wanted to cover himself and show that all was well between husband and wife and convey to us that he just called for a friendly chat."

She added, "In Bruno Campione's defense was the fact that he hired me.   That  did not exempt him from being suspected, though.  I pay attention to everyone, regardless of who foots the bill."

Andi said, "Are you telling me that you picked him as the killer from the very beginning?"

"Certainly not!"

Peter chuckled and said, "In all her cases of investigation, Regula suspects everyone involved as the culprit until proven otherwise!"

His wife said, "Exactly, and this case was no exception. After getting back from my trip to Prescott, Kingman and Albuquerque, I was highly suspicious of Ted Wilson as well as Rocky and Inger Santoro.  It was not until after Elena's body was found and it turned out that she had been pregnant that I concentrated solely on her husband as the murderer."

"Why?" Andi wanted to know.

"I remembered Inger's statement that Bruno had had the mumps as an adult, and I knew this meant there was a good chance that the illness had rendered him sterile. So Bruno's motive of jealousy was much stronger than one of greed for her inheritance would have been. After all, he was already well off. Also, I had a hard time believing that a will in his favor existed. Elena did not strike me as the kind of young woman who would make her will and testament before she even was in possession of the fortune herself."

Peter remarked, "I never met the man, but I got the feeling that Bruno Campione seemed a likable fellow."

"Likable? He was down right lovable, right, Andi?"

Andi's cheeks became as red as her hair when she replied, "You knew I was attracted to him and tried to warn me when we talked on the phone that time. I didn't want to hear it and got mad at you!"

"I remember."

Then Peter said, "He turned out to be a cool and calculating customer. I can't get over how he nonchalantly proceeded to attend the two auctions after killing his wife, and then had the nerve to let the attendant pile his purchases on top of her dead body!"

"Pretty cold blooded," Regula agreed.

As they indulged in their dessert of Bananas Foster New Orleans style, Andi said, "I'm so glad Brenda is okay. That was really clever of her, playing dead."

"She is a resourceful young woman, and it must have taken tremendous willpower on her part to let herself be strangled without trying to fight him off."

Peter asked, "Did anyone ever find out from the estate lawyer where Elena's money is going to end up?"

His wife answered, "I never talked to Mr. Bergstein as it didn't seem necessary after Bruno was caught. However, Brenda volunteered the information when I called to explain why I never arrived at her apartment that day. Elena's trust goes back to her family, with her dad being the number one heir."

He laughed and said, "It'll finance many more of his scientific projects, I'm sure!"

"What'll happen to The Gem?" Andi wondered.

"I suppose someone else will take over the club if there are any assets left after Campione has paid all his attorney bills."

Andi turned to her boss and said, "Remember you told me that love can be a motive for murder? You were referring to David Driscol at the time, but I think it applies to Bruno. He loved Elena but then his love turned into a deranged obsession."

"Yes, I believe you're right."

"And I think Elena loved him. Funny how she insisted that she never had an affair. She even told her sister that the baby was Bruno's."

"I've been dwelling on that fact too."

"Maybe David Driscol only took her dancing and that's all. And what if all the flirting with other guys was just that, flirting."

Regula nodded.

"You reckon Bruno's doctor made a wrong diagnosis and he can produce kids, after all?"

"I'd say that's a possibility."

Andi burst out, "Holy Krewe! He murdered her for no reason!"

# R. A. Huber Mysteries by Alice Zogg

*Final Stop Albuquerque*
*The Fall of Optimum House*
*The Lonesome Autocrat*
*Tracking Backward*
*Turn the Joker Around*
*Reaching Checkmate*

Available at www.amazon.com,
www.barnesandnoble.com
and other online vendors.